A Very British Afterlife

Lee Brown

A Very British Afterlife

Copyright © 2014 Lee Brown

All rights reserved.

ISBN-10: 1500168904
ISBN-13: 978-1500168902

All rights reserved. No part of this publication may be reproduced, stored in a retrieval system, or transmitted, in any form or by any means without the prior written permission of the publisher, nor be otherwise circulated in any form of binding or cover other than that in which it is published and without a similar condition being imposed on the subsequent purchaser.

All characters in this publication are fictitious and any resemblance to real persons, angels or Gods, living or dead, is purely coincidental...honestly.

DEDICATION

For my parents Tom and Olga, who will always be in my heart. My brothers, especially Paul for always caring.

A Very British Afterlife

A Very British Afterlife

CONTENTS

Acknowledgments	I
Foreword	II
IN THE BEGINNING	Pg 1
EXODUS	Pg 13
ACCORDING TO SAINT PETER	Pg 21
ACCORDING TO ARCHANGEL MICHAEL	Pg 28
ACCORDING TO GOD	Pg 41
ACCORDING TO SAINT CHRISTOPHER	Pg 63
ACCORDING TO ARCHANGEL LUCIFER	Pg 81
ACCORDING TO SAINT PAUL	Pg 124
ACCORDING TO SAINT CUTHBERT	Pg 148
ACCORDING TO HARRY	Pg 171
ACCORDING TO SAINT KEYNE	Pg 192
REVELATIONS	Pg 208

A Very British Afterlife

A Very British Afterlife

ACKNOWLEDGMENTS

Helen Creel for being my own angel while writing this book.
Adam Blakemore for his artwork.
Andy Evans and Kylie Davies for their help and encouragement.
Stephen Reader my best friend and greatest support anyone could ever ask for.

FOREWORD

First of all I'd like to take this opportunity to say thank you for reading this book.

Even though this is a story using Christian religion, it is not meant to offend. This is just a story, some of which is true, some of which is fiction, however it's just a story. All it's meant to do is make people smile, laugh maybe even think about how they treat others and their own accomplishments and what greatness people can achieve regardless of what others may think.

So please come in, take a seat, take off your shoes, settle down and enjoy.

A Very British Afterlife

IN THE BEGINNING

As soon as I said those words I knew he would be shocked, they weren't the typical words a friend would say when looking for relationship advice, but I always told it how it was rather than what they want to hear.

"Maybe it's not her, maybe it's you?"

Simon stared at me, his jaw in descent, at a loss for words, but I just shrugged rather than follow it up with anything else that he didn't want to hear.

It was a small café with only seven tables, yet it was friendly and everything on the menu tasted good. The smell of countless fry-ups wafted heavily through the hatch from the kitchen, consuming my concentration and transporting my mind back to my mother's full English breakfast on Sunday mornings when I was a kid.

I did feel a little sorry for Simon. He wasn't a bad person, and he had a heart of gold, not conventionally what you would call good looking but I'd seen a lot worse go out with some stunning women. He just didn't make the most of himself. His jet-black hair was starting to go slightly bald, although his very short haircut only emphasised this. His thick-rimmed glasses detracted from, rather than complimented, his slightly chubby face. Most of the time he dressed smartly and today was no exception, looking marginally out of place against the damp and fading wallpaper in a light grey suit, matching grey tie and purple shirt. But it wasn't his suit that was letting him down most.

Ajinder sat beside him totally oblivious to the conversation, flicking through a hardback book he'd picked up on his way out of the office. He'd bought it from one of those companies that go around businesses selling publications. He was also well dressed, middle-class and fresh out of university. *'Portraits of Famous Leaders through History'* was the title, and he was engrossed within the pages, studying a picture of Adolf Hitler. He'd already finished his pear and Stilton sandwich, the plate pushed to the middle of the table. "You know I think the Holocaust was completely exaggerated."

I looked at him in disbelief. I glanced at Simon to back me up but he was lost in his own world. "You think eleven million was exaggerated? Yeah, you're probably right, those Jewish people are just drama queens." I mocked but Ajinder didn't take any notice.

Simon was a good friend, a truly decent person, who cared for others. Ajinder was just a person I worked with, sat next to and whom invited himself along to lunch time and time again. He annoyed me on the first day we worked together by saying they should sack all the tube drivers for going on strike. He casually brushed off my reply that they were fighting to keep their jobs. He said they should just accept it because he was fed up with them striking and making him late for work.

Simon banged his hand down on our table, condiments shuddering noisily before quickly resettling on the laminate wood. Deep in conversation, and pre-occupied with chasing runny egg round their greasy plates with bread, nobody in the London café even glanced up in acknowledgement.

"But I think she's the one Vince." Simon's words reinforced only a shallow echo of the noise he managed to make a few seconds earlier, but my attention had now snapped back to his dilemma.

"That's great but you said the same about that other girl last month. Sorry to tell you mate, but if she wanted to be with you then she would be with you. We've acknowledged that she likes spending time with you. You get on well and have things in common. You both chat for ages, but face it, at what point does she clam up and go cold?"

"When I talk about wanting a serious relationship and wanting to marry her."

"And how many dates have you actually been on?"

"Four."

"Exactly, don't you think it's a bit heavy, a bit, well, full on? The poor girl just wants to relax, have fun and get to know you and you're turning up with your morning suit and wedding speech prepared. Listen, just lighten up and enjoy it for what it is. If it turns into something then great, if it doesn't then you chalk it up to experience, learn from what went wrong, draw comfort from the fact that at least you tried and that you had a great time with fun memories while you dated. From what you tell me, it wouldn't surprise me if you stood outside her house with a big butterfly net to capture her and put her into a pit you've dug out in your cellar. In fact, I'm surprised you've just had sausage, beans, egg and chips instead of liver, fava beans and a nice Chianti."

He stabbed at the last piece of sausage on his plate just as sharply and forcefully popped it into his mouth. "But I'm 26 and getting old, I'm ready to settle down." I detected the slight shaky frustration in his voice. He was using his fork to enforce most of his words, and on this occasion a small bit of bean juice had landed smack in the centre of his tie. My eyes drawn to it, I then gesture towards the offending item.

"What?" he asked.

"You've got a foreign body on you and I'm not talking about this girl you want to marry." I nodded towards his tie and he looked down. Picking off the bit of food with a finger, he hoovered it into his mouth before then placing the tie in between his lips to suck out the stain.

"You still have most of your life ahead of you Si. Your time will come but don't force it mate. Every relationship especially at the beginning should just be about one sentence - let's see how it goes."

He reluctantly pushed his plate away and leant on the table. "So, what do you think I should do?"

"Maybe play hard to get for a while, give her the space she's asked for, text her when you're doing something fun to let her know you have your own life. That her decisions won't stop you from living and enjoying yourself. Let her miss you or more to the point, let her realise that she can miss you."

"Do I tell her I wish she was there?"

"NO! That's the whole point, you're letting her

know you can still have fun without her."

Even though I was saying the words I could tell he wasn't really listening or getting the point because it wasn't what he wanted to hear. It was true, my advice did seem counter-intuitive; if you want something then you go for it, you don't hold back. When it comes to dating it was different, I knew even now he would spoil it for himself and lose her.

"George Bush", Ajinder spoke up again.

"Oh, he's back", I feigned surprise. "What?"

He turned the book to show me a picture of George Bush Junior. "George Bush. Hey, do you know what they do with the American presidents to make them do what they want?"

"Who?" I asked.

"The people who really control America. What they do is they drug them, totally strip them and take photographs of them with prostitutes so that they can blackmail them into doing what they want."

I shake my head. "You'd think that people wouldn't become president if they knew that was going to happen to them."

"Oh, they don't know it's going to happen."

"Hang on", I said. "So, let me get this right. You know that this stuff happens to the presidents of the United States but the statesmen in America don't. You'd think that a middle-class, British computer programmer would be one of the last people to find out about stuff like that."

"Incredible, isn't it?" Ajinder asked, surprised.

"Oh, amazing", I replied sarcastically.

"Just like 9/11. That was all an inside job. You see the people who control America wanted a war with Afghanistan and Iraq because they wanted the oil, so that's why they did it."

"So they murdered thousands of their own people, affected their own economy and damaged their tourism just because they wanted to start a war. Wouldn't it have been easier to destroy the Statue of Liberty?" The scepticism was evident within my voice but Ajinder continued to flick through his book.

Simon shifted his body, his arm making an abstract design in the gravy in preparation of the call for action. "I'll ask the waitress."

"She'll just tell you the same as me", I told him as I caught her eye. She smiled and walked over.

"Can I get you anything else Vincent?" she asked, her Eastern European accent still unmistakable. She was a lovely girl, early twenties, blonde, slim, beautiful and she was so friendly, always smiling and I didn't even have to ask for an order these days; she instantly knew what I wanted. She was a girl who believed in love, she married young and even had her husband's name tattooed up her forearm in some foreign language. I'd been getting to know her over the last few months; I knew she was devoted to her husband. She'd fallen for him because he was a bad-boy and because of that, she was perfect to tell Simon how it was.

"I'm fine thank you, but he has a question for you."

"Okay, if I can answer I will." She grinned a grin that meant that she was enjoying the attention. This was a consultation that was affording her the chance to not just be a waitress if only for a few moments.

"Okay, so if a girl says she just wants space, would you give her space or pursue her?" Simon asked.

Her eyes moved to the top corner of her face and

she moved her pen to her lips while she thought of her answer. "If she wants space I'd give her space. Sometimes if you try to make someone do something, they do the opposite. Okay, did that help?"

"Yes, thank you", I said.

She smiled, fluttered her eyelashes and raised her head slightly as if she had just received a pat on the head. With a slight bow, she moved off to serve a group of four customers who had just taken their seats at another table.

Ajinder called her back asking if they had any free hand sanitisation products. When she said no he said: "It's okay, I have to touch the coins in my pocket and the door handle so I'll use my own when I leave." She looked at me confused and I shook my head slightly, acknowledging that she should just ignore him. She then moved back to serving the next table.

"Do you think I should send her flowers?" Simon asked.

I hit him on the head with a folded napkin. "Haven't you been listening to a single thing we've said? If she wants to be with you and it's a special occasion then send her a bouquet but if she doesn't want to be with you, sending her flowers isn't going to change her mind."

"Cheers mate, I owe you one."

"You don't owe me a thing, I'm a mate and that's what friends are for."

"I wish I was in control of my relationships as much as I was in control of my staff."

"That is just so wrong on so many levels. You don't want to control a relationship, it should be equal, and after all I thought you wanted a girlfriend not a puppet."

"Hmmm", he replied sounding unconvinced. "Anyway it's okay for you; you have someone you've been with for ages."

I shook my head. "It hasn't always been like that, I've been out with a lot of girls before finding Jennifer, from lawyers to dancers, from English to Japanese. Before I met her I didn't just settle for anyone, my search was meticulous. By the time I did meet her I knew exactly what I was looking for and knew she was perfect for me."

"But you didn't want to stay with any of the others? That's bullshit!"

"No, because it never felt right, it felt good at the beginning but the honeymoon period never lasts and you're left with something that can either be amazing or the loneliest place in the world. With Jennifer, it was so different. I actually felt complete, the relationship never felt one sided, I wanted to share things with her, to open up to her. God, as cliché as it may sound, I even want kids with her."

"How did you know?"

I shrugged. "I just did, it never felt like a chore, just normal. She was everything I'd looked for; funny, cool, intelligent, and sexy and we had fun together. We laughed a lot, we discovered things together; new places, new tastes, hell, I think we even discovered a lot about ourselves. But she also scares me. It scares me that one day I might be without her."

"Now, Margaret Thatcher, she was a great leader." Ajinder smiled at a picture of her in his book. I picked up the fork from my plate and gestured that I was going to jab him in the head with it. Simon let out a small laugh.

"Just think though, tomorrow at this time you'll be on holiday with her, kicking back and having some fun", said Simon, as I placed the fork back down.

I picked up my cup and downed the last of my tea, enjoying the taste and thinking how I'll miss it when I go. "Even that scares me to death, asking the girl of my dreams to be my wife is a once in a lifetime event, it has to be the perfect time, the perfect words and that's even before the nerves of her saying 'yes', or 'no', or even worse, just going quiet and saying nothing."

"You are good together", Simon nodded.

"Thanks, she does believe in me, she knows that I deserve the best of everything in life. She wants me to get out of I.T. and do something with people. I never ever felt like I fit in anywhere. Sure, I made friends easily wherever I went; I like to think I'm a decent bloke and I love to make people laugh, for the simple reason that laughter is happiness, even if it's for just a brief few seconds that you are bringing real, genuine, pure happiness to them. I guess I'm very much my father's son, he was like that."

"What do you mean?"

"At his funeral, someone said that he could walk into a pub that was full of non-English speaking foreigners and by the time he walked out everyone would be calling him 'mate'. She knows that my skills are being wasted, especially in this job I'm in now, and I should be doing something else. You know what, for the first time in my life I feel that things might actually be working out and falling into place for me. I have a great apartment, Okay, it is only rented but I still love it, it feels like home, when nowhere felt like home in the last 10 years and now I have Jennifer. All the hard work, pain and sacrifices I made in life weren't in vain. Most of the time, I have to admit, when things became rough, I thought I was getting payback for the bad things I did when I was younger. Speaking of pain and suffering, I need to get back to work. My boss is doing my appraisal this afternoon."

It's always in the eyes, I thought, as he stared at me across the desk. As much as I was able to read people by their behaviour or words, people with no emotion in their eyes still unnerved me to death. My manager stared at me, a big man very, very, very out of shape. He was a typical computer geek at heart and if you had Jabba the Hutt and took away all his charisma, charm and friendliness you would be at least some way to describing this man.

"I still have a problem with you", he said, with no sadness or happiness in his voice nor emotion in his face. "That last job I gave you took you longer than I said it would."

"But you didn't know anything about the system!"

"I know."

"Or the database."

"I know."

"You didn't know how muddled the old system was programmed. I had to work it out before I could rebuild it; no one explained anything to me."

"I know."

"But you knew it would only take six weeks."

"Correct."

"How did you come to that conclusion?"

"Well, there was a lot of finger in the air guesstimates."

"And that's why you're having a go at me because your guess was wrong."

"Regardless of that I need to know that I can trust you with these jobs, I need someone professional."

"Hang on a minute; I've come to work, even when I'm ill. I've never taken any holiday since I started; I've tried to get that job done as soon as possible. I didn't get a specification, because you said I had to create it. I had to write my own from a five minute meeting about a system no one knows anything about. Then, when I asked if there was anything I needed to know about it, I got no reply from the management. Instead, you called me an f'ing retard to my own director. When I emailed you and the director saying that it needed to be planned with timelines and milestones discussed, you summoned me into a room and called me a troublemaker. You don't speak to me on a day-to-day basis even though I only sit two seats away from you. No one can even get a good morning from you. I work next to a guy who has several years' knowledge of this place but when you ask him anything he behaves like he has permanent Premenstrual Tension and talks down to anyone who isn't a manager. He's the only person I've met who does put the 'I' in team. Yet you say I'm the one that's unprofessional. You didn't go to the Nazi school of management did you?"

He tilted his head back slightly, his lip curled at

one side and he stared.

I challenged him again: "You know back in the day, people followed leaders because of their virtues, whether Christian, like kindness, sympathy, love or Pagan such as assertiveness, heroism, leadership or confidence. These days problems start because those chosen to lead can lock themselves up in a room and knock work out by themselves; no virtues necessary, no people skills required. It's bosses like you who destroy a company from within, yet people turn a blind eye to it because you're a manager."

He slightly sneered: "And I demand your respect so I will tell you that you need to change your attitude otherwise you will be looking for a new job."

"Threats as well, glad we had this talk to build my enthusiasm and bolster my morale." Some people had asked me in the past if I had a problem with authority as if I was some technical rebel without a cause. In truth it was the way I was mismanaged, ignored and never considered to discuss or plan projects I worked on. The management just wanted a machine to agree and just get on with things regardless.

"Send the next person in", he said, as I started to gather several pages of my appraisal form from the table between us. "Oh, and I know one thing about history, Rome did not create an empire by having an appraisal - they did it by destroying those who opposed them."

And for the first time in the meeting a smile appeared on his face.

EXODUS

A golden statue glinted in the midday sunlight beside a very ornate Buddhist temple within the Chiang Mai Province of Thailand. A few tourists stood back taking photos of the beautiful scenery and also of locals lighting candles that were placed upon the ground in front of the statue.

Jennifer and I walked out of the temple hand in hand. I caught a glimpse of my reflection across the shiny, golden door. Okay, I was an ordinary-looking guy, slim, brown hair, blue eyes, nothing special, but when I caught a glimpse of Jennifer's reflection it was like I was seeing her for the first time. She was beautiful. Her hand found mine and I lifted it and kissed the soft skin between her middle and forefinger. "Thank you for this. Coming here was one of my dreams. It's on my bucket list, one of my things to do before I die and you've helped make it come true. I feel so lucky to have found you", I said.

She took a step closer and kissed me on the lips, she smiled, looking deeply into my eyes "Shhh, you don't have to thank me. It's my job to make your dreams come true. I still remember you talking about wanting to come here on our first date."

"Really!"

"Of course, it was the best date I'd ever had. No one had been so romantic to me before and it was fun. Having lunch at the highest restaurant in London. Going to see a theatre show in the afternoon, then listening to the carol singers around the Christmas tree in Trafalgar Square while drinking hot chocolate, it was fabulous. Anyway if you're finished looking at yourself in the reflection I have something to tell you." I leant into her. She tenderly put her hands at either side of my head. I smiled and got ready for a kiss, feeling her soft lips upon mine quickly followed by a massive lick from her soft wet tongue, from my lips all the way up my face to my forehead. I take a tissue from my pocket and quickly wipe my face and she immediately starts to laugh. Her laugh.

That was the laugh that made me fall for her, it wasn't her looks, even though she was attractive, and had a great personality; she was one of the few truly nice, genuine people you meet in life. But her laugh, it wasn't an odd laugh like someone sawing a piece of wood, or like a donkey, but it wasn't a normal one either. The only way I could ever describe it was a closed-mouth giggle, a giggle that I'd never tire of. I loved making her laugh; to me it felt like evidence that I was making her happy. Sometimes when you've gone through so much bad in your life and something or someone good shows it's hard to believe that it's in your life, you almost look for evidence of why.'

"Oh, like that is it?" I grabbed hold of her arms.

"Yeah, that's exactly how it is." She laughed as she struggled, guessing what was about to happen. Trying to wriggle out of my grasp I lick all the way up her left arm.

"Urgh...your suntan lotion tastes horrible. I'll get you back at the hotel, don't you worry, and I'll give you such a licking young lady."

Her eyebrows rose with a smile. "Oh, promises promises", she said cheekily. Her face moved closer to mine for another kiss, which was promptly interrupted by both of us backing into some poor Taiwanese lady minding her business. We both apologised to her the best we could using gestures, hoping they would bridge our communication barrier. We gave each other an embarrassed look as we quickly walked away.

I looked at the beautiful, slim, blonde girl, in her early thirties, the same age as me, and smiled to myself, a smile that today I wanted to share with the world. I wanted to take that smile, replicate it and pass it on to everyone I met and for them to do likewise.

We looked at each other and grinned, realising that we both stood out a mile amongst the people around us, as we were the only ones with pink skin, typical British people abroad, not used to the hot weather.

I turned on the spot while looking at the vision around us, taking it all in. It was so breathtaking I couldn't believe it wasn't a dream. The smell of incense wafting in the slight breeze, and the sun beating down upon my face. This felt like a perfect moment, my perfect moment in life. It's times like these, which stay with you forever, that keep you going through the difficult days with the hope that there will be more days like this.

"This place is beautiful", we said simultaneously and then laughed. We had both been known to say the same thing at the same time. She always said this was one of the first things that attracted her to me; to her it was a sign that we were both on the same wavelength. She had confessed this to me at intimate moments, to mutual friends in the past at dinner parties, and several times when she was drunk.

"So, have you thought about what I said?" Jennifer asked.

"I don't know, it's a big step, I've already changed my direction in life once."

"Yes, but you are so wasted in I.T."

"I know", I replied, "but at least it's a safe-ish job, the world will always need programmers."

"Yeah, but you're more of a people person. You should become a teacher or a nurse, you have a great bedside manner and that's a skill in its own."

"A teacher with a great bedside manner, you know, you can get in trouble for that these days", I said, trying to be flippant.

"Oh, you know what I mean. How many I.T. jobs have you had in the last few years and you keep coming across the same problem? Managers that don't actually want to work with people; they'd be happier with a robot they can feed their imperfect specifications into, wait a short time until the robot produces the perfect application with the least amount of effort or input by them. They don't even train people, rather just expect them to know everything. Not realising that people have different levels of experience and knowledge. They don't want to deal with people, especially not people with a personality."

"I know, but…"

"And don't you keep saying that I.T. these days is just full of three types of asses: assholes, ass lickers and Aspergers? That they themselves think that just because they have knowledge about something everyone else should have the same knowledge? That the industry is full of closed minded, unenlightened, conceited robots?"

"I know, but it's a safe job and without a job that pays okay we wouldn't have been able to afford this holiday. Anyway, swiftly changing the subject, what do you think of this place?"

She pursed her lips, while shaking her head half in frustration with me and half in jest.

"It is so amazing Vince; it has to be the best place I've ever visited, so spiritual, it's breathtaking." Her eyes were alight with the enthusiasm she always lived her life by. She then grasped both of my hands in hers.

"Teach me some words, Vince. What is the Thai word for Temple?"

"What."

"The Thai word for Temple", she repeated.

"What is the Thai word for Temple", I said, playfully.

"That's what I'm asking."

"What."

"I'm asking what is the Thai word for Temple?"

"That's right."

"But I haven't said anything!" Jennifer said shaking her head, closing her eyes as she does while grinning her full grin, which to me lit up the area more than the sun beaming off the golden statues nearby.

"What is the Thai word for Temple?"

"That's what I asked you."

"But I said what", I said.

"And I asked you what's the word."

"The Thai word for Temple."

"Yes, so are you going to tell me?" she said, sticking her tongue out at me.

"What."

"What is the Thai word for Temple?"

"Yeah, that's right, the Thai name for Temple is what, but spelt WAT, you dummy." I pushed her a little in a playful manner.

"You geek", she said and pounced on me, wrapping her arms around my neck whilst laughing then peppered my face with kisses. "Thank you, Vince; you've shown me that sharing life with you is what makes life special, so special I think I'll even do a Snoopy dance." She tilted her head so that she was looking at the sky and started to do a kind of Riverdance, jog thing on the spot.

"I know petal. Listen, I wanted to bring you here to ask you something." I paused, then laughed, trying to hide my nervousness of the question that had been behind this whole holiday. I'd let three days go by just waiting for somewhere as awe-inspiring as this location, just so it would be extra special, something we'd both remember for the rest of our lives.

"Oh really, Mr?" she said stopping her dance, then I saw her face become distracted and she was looking past me. "Oh my God, look Vincent, my favourite."

I turned to see a local monk holding an elephant on a length of rope, patting it lovingly.

"Wow, Vince look at the size of it, must be about nine foot tall, and look at its tusks, they are huge. Oh, I know what, I'll take your photo with them then you can take some of me."

"But I need to ask you something, besides, they're your favourite, not mine", I said, thinking at least it buys me some extra time to build up the courage. The elephant did smell a bit, but then again I bet the monks don't really have a supply of Molton Brown they use to constantly bathe their animals in, or deodorant to spray them with. Perhaps there's a gap in the market; body spray for animals, now even your pets can smell fresh and sexy … can pets be sexy? Perhaps pets shouldn't be sexy, maybe it is a moral thing, after all there are far too many perverts around these days without them now giving your pets the come-on.

The elephant's trunk sniffed towards me as I walked up to it, patting it on the side of the head.

"Are you hungry boy, are you?" I asked this marvellous animal while pulling a handful of nuts out of a packet from my trouser pocket and feeding him. I'd purchased the nuts from a store close to our hotel that morning in case we'd see any monkeys to feed, we hadn't as yet, but this animal was now receiving the benefits.

Click. Jen took a picture of me and the elephant in action.

"Jennifer", I said, still feeding the elephant.

"Yes, honey."

Click. Another photo.

"You know I love you, don't you?"
"Yes Vincent, you know I do."
Click. Another photo.
"I want to ask you something …"
Click. And another.
"Yes, darling", she said, emotion now in her voice, I guessed she knew what I was about to ask. "You can ask me anything you want, and I promise to capture whatever you say on camera so that it will last forever and ever in time, just like my love for you."

I turned around and looked directly into her eyes.
"Jennifer, will you marry me?"
Click.
Darkness.

ACCORDING TO SAINT PETER

I pushed open the glass door in front of me and walked into an office. An office? Where's the elephant? Where's the temple? And, for that matter, where was Jennifer?

The office was clean, with white walls and beige-coloured furnishings, which included seats in the middle positioned around a glass coffee table with an assortment of magazines upon it. A glass hatch and a door were built into the opposite end of the room, which led to a further office. A young woman, maybe in her late 20s, sat reading a magazine. She looked up at me, smiled and said hello. I tried to raise a smile but, because I was still trying to work out how I got here, it came out as a grimace and she turned her head, continuing with what she was reading.

I walked around the back of the woman towards the hatch and touched the back of her chair to make sure this wasn't some kind of dream. It felt real. But I didn't understand how I had got there. I looked down at the girl as I passed; the magazine she was reading was a cooking magazine, with a recipe for angel cake written in English. Well at least I'm in an English-speaking country, wouldn't know what I'd do if I were somewhere else. I was hopeless at getting by in different countries, I always felt so stupid and lazy when I went anywhere and couldn't even speak a little bit of the local language. I once went to Germany and thought I could remember enough from my school days to order a glass of orange juice and a beer, only for the barmaid to pull different faces at me to show that she didn't understand a word I was saying. After the third time of me repeating my order and her almost walking away, a guy sitting at the bar told her what I wanted in English and, in a broad Australian accent, she asked why I didn't just say that in the first place. That was the start and end of me trying to integrate with the locals on that holiday.

It could still be a dream though. I could have grabbed the girl and kissed her, then if she slapped me I would know it was not a dream, but if it wasn't a dream then we'd both feel pretty bad. It's not a great first impression: making people think that you're a sex pest. I could have ended up being arrested, which also put an end to my next idea of smashing the place up.

I noticed the man at the hatch as I wandered over, still not knowing what I was going to say. '*Hi, who are you and where am I?*' would just sound mad.

"Hello there, can I have your name please?" he said in a slightly raised voice, so that it could be heard through the hatch.

Bugger, I thought, do I give him a false name or my real name? What if I'm not meant to be here, wherever here is? What happens if it's some government experiment I've escaped from and inadvertently wandered back into and I'll get tested on again? I've seen an American TV series where stuff like that happened. Could something like that really happen? I looked down at my hands, half expecting and half hoping that claws would slide out between my knuckles. Nothing happened, so I'm not a mutant. Oh well, I guess I'll give him my name.

"Yea ... yes, it's Vincent", I said.

"And your surname please?" he asked.

"D ... D ... Dabney." I turned around to see the girl in the chair looking up at me.

"Hello", she said again with a relaxed and pleasant look on her face.

"Hmm", I replied, half sullenly and half embarrassed, and turned back to the man, who searched down a list attached to the clipboard.

"Now, let's see, Vince ... Vince ..." He turned over the sheet of paper he was searching from and read down that side. "Oh, erm ... hold on, I'll just make a phone call." He walked away from the window to a desk behind him, picked up a telephone receiver, dialled a number and held a conversation with the unseen person on the other side of the line. I listened to see if I could gather any information of where I was.

"Hi, that is Personnel isn't it? Sorry I didn't recognise your voice, it's Peter from Reception here. How's your first week going? Are you enjoying it there? Yeah, they are a good bunch. Listen, I have a new starter just come in but I can't find him on the list, are we expecting any late entries? No problem, I'll hold."

He looked up at me: "Sorry for the wait, it shouldn't take too long."

I nodded, intrigued that he had said "new starter". New starter for what? An office job? I looked at him in his suit, then back at the woman, who was also wearing a suit, then down at what I was wearing; yip, I was still wearing my holiday clothes, cotton beige trousers, short-sleeved dark blue shirt and flip-flops - hardly office wear. Plus, I couldn't remember leaving my old job and getting excited about a new one. I leaned on the counter, rubbing my head and trying to desperately remember the gap in my memory. I hadn't touched alcohol for years but even when I did drink I never used to forget anything. Some people used to 'get off' with dodgy-looking people they had picked up on a night out and conveniently sworn that it was 'just with the drink,' and they couldn't remember anything the following day.

"Hi, what ... none at all? Oh, ah ... that's a problem then. Tell you what, would you do me a favour, could you have a look for a Mr Vincent Dabney ... yes ... English ... Oh really, yeah it's just we've got a guy here who's not on the list. Listen, I've got a lot of new starters coming in soon. Yes, what to do? Tell you what, can you ask your boss to pop down when he has a spare minute and I'll try and sort this out? Great, thank you, ta-ta for now."

I looked up and watched Peter put the phone back down and take a deep breath as he walked towards the door in the separating wall and opened it.

"Mr Dabney", he said. "Would you mind following me please?"

Oh no, this doesn't look good I thought. Hesitantly, I followed him to the other side of the office and into a smaller room built in the side of the bigger one. The room was little but it comfortably fitted two three-seater cream sofas, separated by a glass table.

"Please have a seat Mr Dabney", Peter said as he closed the door behind me. I sat down on the seat closest to the door whilst Peter sat on the sofa opposite. He placed the clipboard down onto the glass table, crossed his legs and clutched his hands together. Odd body language. I started to feel like James Bond about to be interrogated by some evil villain with physical traits like metal claws as hands, metal teeth, electronic wheels instead of feet or an eye of a badger.

"Not very nice weather we're having at the moment. I'm not sure about an Arab Spring but I do think it's going to be a Shiite Summer." I said, trying to make some kind of light conversation, but he just stared at me for a few moments, which led into an uncomfortable silence, with Peter still staring.

"Okay now, first thing I have to tell you is … you are not on my list, which makes all this a bit tricky really, as you really … well you really shouldn't be here", he said. No time for pleasantries then, I thought.

"Okay", I said calmly and slowly, looking confused as if he was explaining the most complicated bit of rocket science. "But I don't know where I am", I shrugged, irritation starting to creep into my voice. They can't blame this on me, it's not like I came here on purpose; I didn't ask to come here.

"Yes, exactly which brings me on to my second point …"

There was a knock on the door and a handsome man in his late twenties, clean-shaven, blonde shoulder length hair, wearing a yellow robe and carrying a manila folder entered the room. He smiled a big white beaming smile. He seemed to have an air of friendliness about him.

"Hello Michael, thanks for coming down", Peter said in a voice that sounded relieved that he wasn't alone with me anymore.

"Hello all", Michael said in a confident voice, nodding his head, his long hair bouncing around his face. "No problem, anything to help." His big wide grin was almost infectious. He sounded more surfer than office management. I guessed this was the person Peter had requested to come down on the previous phone call.

Peter looked over and pointed to me.

"Michael, I'd like you to meet Vincent. Vincent this is Michael, he's the head of Personnel."

I stood up and shook Michael's hand, his big fists almost smothering mine, I half expected an over-aggressive, tight grasp but it was as friendly and enthusiastic as he was.

"Hello, very nice to meet you", Michael grinned.

It did put me at ease, slightly … I mean no place that was bad or wrong could ever have someone like this working here, could they? But who were these people? How did I get here? No one was expecting me but why should they? But if I am here why aren't they expecting me? And why was that blonde guy wearing a dress? I tried to stop my mind from racing and listen to what they were saying; otherwise I was bound to miss something important. It was always like that at university, I'd sit there taking notes trying to follow what was being said and then I'd have a slight lapse in concentration and I'd miss something really important and not have a clue what they were going on about after that … Oh, there I go again! CONCENTRATE! I shouted to myself. I grinned and sat back down on the comfortable sofa.

Okay, I thought, what would James Bond do if he was in a room with two strange guys and wanted information from them? Karate chop them in the windpipe and torture them? Maybe that idea should be left alone at this moment and maybe it was time to go to Plan B; ask them a few questions and try to read their body language to see if they were hiding anything from me.

"Okay, I'm worried now, there's two of you and you're being cagey, so I feel like you are about to tell me some bad news." I laughed nervously.

Both Michael and Peter remained silent and then looked at each other. This, I admitted silently to myself, I did not like one bit.

Michael shifted uncomfortably in his seat, screwed his eyes shut while his head sank down briefly, he then opened them and looked me directly in the face. "Well no, not bad news exactly … you see, you're dead."

ACCORDING TO ARCHANGEL MICHAEL

I sank back into the sofa as if a great weight had landed upon me. I'm sure I must have misheard.

"I'm what?!" I said.

"Dead, deceased ... erm, how did Monty Python say it? 'You are no more, you have shuffled off the mortal coil, joined the choir invisible'." Michael laughed. "Oh, we love that sketch up here, we've got one of them here, 'course we always get him to do that for us, we never get sick of it."

I shook my head in disbelief. First he tells me I'm dead, now he was going on about Monty bloody Python. They didn't seem too bothered about my misfortune. I held my hand up to stop Michael just before he was about to continue.

"Hold on, you tell me that it's not exactly bad news and then you tell me I'm dead." I closed my eyes and covered my face with both hands, shaking my head. "This can't be true, I feel alive, I can feel my skin. Surely this is all just some mistake, there must be something I or someone could do?"

Michael clicked his fingers: "Hey, let's not dwell

upon the negative, let's look at the positive … it's not all bad news, it's quite nice up here."

"It was quite nice down there, and what do you mean I'm not on your list?" I could feel my voice starting to get louder; my patience was now wearing thin.

"Ah yes, well, now according to our records", Peter's voice sounding very clinical, like a born civil servant who loved explaining red tape at the drop of a hat. "That is a bit of a problem. You see, not being on the list means that you've come here before your time … I bet you were a nice, decent person on Earth?"

"Yeah, I tried to be."

"They always say the good die young", Peter chuckled. He looked at Michael then shifted his gaze to me, who was not laughing, in fact just the opposite, I was almost ready to leap across the table and throttle him. Maybe it's time for Plan A now and I karate chop his windpipe. Not sure if he could read my mind or could just tell by the look on my face, but he abruptly stopped, clearing his throat in a false way, trying to disguise the laugh.

"Yes, well…we have to say it's not the first time this has happened."

"Oh really?" I said, the sarcasm being evident from my tone. I felt my temper simmering like a pan of chicken soup that wasn't very good for the soul and just any minute now they were going to turn the heat up slightly too much and it will come bubbling over.

"Yes, there was Christopher Reeve, Steve Irwin, Cleopatra and then there was John Lennon; he wasn't supposed to have gone that early either."

"That's right Peter", Michael said. "Yeah, terrible,

he was supposed to have outlived the other Beatles. He's still heartbroken, hates being away from Yoko and can't wait till she passes so they can be reunited. Of course that wasn't animal related, that was an administrative error."

Peter nodded in agreement "Yes poor Haniel, making a mistake like that, although he didn't seem too bothered I would be absolutely mortified. Well you would be wouldn't you?"

Yet again, I felt exasperated that these two were not helping me with this serious problem. I interrupted.

"If you two don't mind stopping to chat about your wander down incompetence lane and tell me that this is just a joke or a dream or something." Again I searched their faces and body language for some glimmer of a smile so I'd know that this was all just a joke, but there was none.

"Sorry but I'm afraid not, Vince. This is it, your mortal form is over and you're in the afterlife", Peter said with a shrug.

"But I swear to God I'm an Atheist. Well, I'm sorry but I can't believe it", I said bringing my right fist down into the palm of my left hand, then crossing my arms in defiance.

"Yes I know, it does take some getting used to, dude; it is a bit of a shock to the system. The only thing we can do to convince you is to show you, I suppose", said Michael said, who by now wasn't smiling but wide-eyed. He somehow still looked enthusiastic.

I shook my head as if nothing could convince me that I'd died. "Show me what exactly?"

"Good question", Michael said. He thought for a

few seconds. "Your funeral maybe, would that help? Seeing all your friends and family mourning your passing?"

Wow, this was getting very serious. I guess that would prove that this was real, but would it convince me? I guess it couldn't hurt, if these people wanted to prove to me so badly that I was dead then it could be possible that I was in the afterlife.

"Maybe it would help."

Michael gave me a thumbs up. "Dude, I'm gonna have to get an HEV12 signed off by the boss, then we can pop down and pay our respects…to…you."

"Your boss?" I said.

He's not going to say who I think he's going to say is he?

"Yes, you know, the Managing Director … the boss … God." Michael said the word 'God' as if he'd just said 'socks', 'crisps' or 'Bognor Regis'.

Yip, he really did. "What, really? God?" I asked, my jaw almost hanging wide open.

"Yes, He's the only one that can sign off this stuff, this may be the afterlife but we do still have rules and regulations, otherwise it would be absolute chaos. You know, I am still surprised the way people get shocked when I mention his name, although I guess it's because I've known him for so long. He's always been my boss and I just take it for granted."

"I remember when I first met him", Peter said, nodding in acknowledgment to Michael's last remark. "It was such a big thing, but He was just my best chum's father and you always want to impress your friend's parents don't you?"

Michael nodded: "He's a decent guy really, just like everyone else, He can have his good and bad days."

"Will I get to meet him?" I asked.

Michael's face lit up. "Definitely, he'll want to see you, especially after you've come up a bit early."

I hoped he didn't think he was finally getting through to me because I was still going to need a whole lot of convincing that this wasn't just some figment of my imagination. I should imagine I'll soon meet up with Salvador Dali wearing a melted clock for a hat and riding a penguin next.

"How early? How much of my life has been taken away from me?" I asked.

Michael opened up the Manila folder within his hands and skim read through the top page.

"Well the official date is in about 35 years time … But that could change at any time, you know, with free will and stuff. You could just decide one day to step in front of a bus, jump off a cliff, or feed yourself to a tiger."

"Oh, tricky thing, free will", Peter agreed and looked up at the ceiling. I guessed that he was remembering incidents in the past, maybe where free will had some major influence in people's lives that he had met or witnessed.

Michael nodded again. "Definitely, that's why the M.D. wasn't so keen on it in the early days, too much upkeep and hard work. Well, that's why He created us to manage the souls that do the admin. The more people are born into the world the more upkeep it needs, and the more we need extra admin."

I felt the warmth of anger quickly rising through my body, slowly building up from my feet to a crescendo out of my mouth.

"So, you're telling me I've been cheated out of half of my life?"

"Well, I wouldn't say cheated. Remember, you are not on our list, so we didn't plan it. What was the last thing you remember before getting here?" Michael asked.

I tried to compile my last thoughts before I entered the office.

"Erm, I was on holiday in Thailand with my girlfriend and we were outside this Buddhist temple. I saw an elephant, it was absolutely massive, and it looked … well, a bit sad, just chained up like that. I started to feed it some nuts I had on me and I turned around to ask my girlfriend … something." I really didn't feel like going into details and sharing what I was actually going to ask her, not the way I was feeling at the moment. I certainly didn't want to share something so nice and personal with two people that had just given me the worst news of my life … death … whatever. "Then that was it, next thing I knew I was wandering in here." I grabbed my shirt, trying to show them evidence to prove my story. "Look, I'm still in my holiday clothes."

"Yeah, Vincent, just a piece of advice. Maybe not a good idea to wear that shirt." Michael said, shaking his head and squinting as he pointed at me.

"Why? I like this shirt, my girlfriend bought it for me."

"No, nothing wrong with your clothes. Just, with your name being Vincent Dabney … Maybe you shouldn't wear monogrammed shirts…especially up here."

"Oh, I never thought about that. Yeah, she actually bought it as a joke and bet me money that I wouldn't wear it. I did tell her she's the one that has to be seen with me, the joke is on her as much as it was on me ... sorry", I said, self-conscious I might have embarrassed the people in front of me.

Peter waved his hand to show that what I said wasn't necessary. "No, please don't apologise, just thought I'd warn you more than anything. I'm not sure I have anything here in your size but I'm sure I have something in lost property we can slip you into. You will be getting changed into a robe anyway sooner or later. The M.D. is very big on robes up here. When you're away from here it's dress-down but all will be explained in the handbook you'll be provided with."

"Handbook ... in the afterlife, really?" I asked.

Michael nodded: "Yeah we in Personnel have a handbook, you know, rules and regulations. What goes on etc, etc. I'm sure most of it you will learn as time goes on."

"Anyway we still haven't found out how you died", Peter said, butting into the conversation while clapping his hands together. "I'm intrigued now, I must admit. I do like a good mystery. It's quite like a 'who done it'. A bit like Columbo. I used to love that programme. You know, I used to pop down to Earth when I could and watch episodes. I used to have to make excuses so I could get down there of course, we can't just pop down to watch TV. He used to pretend he was thick but he wasn't really, brilliant. I was never sure about Quincy; he was only a police pathologist but he used to go out trying to solve the crimes. If I was a detective working on the case I would tell him to simply bugger off and let the police do their job and he should get back to the lab instead of letting that poor Asian man do all the hard work—"

"My death ..." I interrupted.

"Oh yes." Peter blinked his eyes a few times, as if being snapped out of some hypnotic dream. "Yes, we are going have to ask the M.D. … Sorry, God, about that."

"What, because He's omnipresent?" I nodded, expecting them to agree with me. I wasn't a total novice about religions; I'd been about and had learned a lot from different places and times within my past. There were times I had attended church when I was younger, information I'd collected on sightseeing tours on different holidays, and of course facts I'd picked up from books or pub quizzes.

Peter sparked up as if he had caught me out, like he was solving a crime, playing the part of Columbo.

"Erm, no, you see, a lot of people make the mistake of thinking that. He can't be everywhere at once, but then again who can?"

I nodded in agreement but then thought about it for a second and raised an index finger.

"Chris Evans the English television and radio presenter was close to it at one point, or so it felt like."

"Yeah, we were glad we never had a TV or radio up here at that point … we literally did thank God for small mercies in those years", Michael said, nodding and looking into the distance, reminiscing about that particular time.

"Hey, but hold on, if I remember correctly, it's written in the Bible that God … sorry, your M.D. was … is, omnipresent?"

"Yes, it does a few times", Peter said. "One being Jeremiah 23:23,24.

"Am I a God at hand, saith the Lord, and not a God afar off? Can any hide himself in secret places that I shall not see him? Saith the Lord. Do not I fill heaven and Earth? Saith the Lord."

But the truth is … He's not. You see that's where Saints come into it, they observe and report back. Oh, He fully intended to keep an eye on everything, but you know what it's like with a baby. You put it down and turn your back for a second and by the time you've turned back around they are feeding toast to your DVD player or colouring the dog in with a crayon."

"Well, that's how the whole Garden of Eden thing started", Michael said, shuffling slightly uncomfortably in his seat. His voice turned into a whisper: "You see, if He was everywhere, he would have stopped the snake from chatting to Adam and Eve. Instead, he turned his back and by the time he'd turned around everything had gone tits up."

I almost choked, shocked at hearing profanity, as slight as it was, in heaven. "Oh yeah, he was furious, spitting mad he was." His head almost mimicking a spitting motion when mentioning the word. He looked into the glass table with a far-off, almost glazed, expression.

"He does have a bit of a temper, nice bloke though", he said, more to himself than to me.

"Yes, quite right. Here, let me look at that, I need your dress size for the robes, if we have any in your size down here. If not, you will be outfitted soon enough." Peter took the Manila folder from Michael and ran his finger down the first page, nodded to himself, closed it, handed it back and hurried out of the room. Michael and I followed slowly behind as we walked back into the main office.

"Look, I'm really sorry, I really am but I'm still not

too sure this isn't just a dream, so can we go and get this sorted out so that I can either wake up or you can prove to me that this is real." I felt as though I was wasting everyone's time, which was silly if it was my own dream. These two seemed decent guys, just doing their job. They hadn't been horrible to me and seemed just as clueless about me being here as I was.

"Of course we can get this sorted, hey, and don't be sorry, you haven't done anything wrong. I also need to complete your folder I suppose. Look, I'm sorry; I wish I could make this easier for you Vincent."

"Is that the folder of my life? My entire life from when I was born until the day I … well, until today. All my details, good and bad?" I asked.

"Just the highlights, really, the good and bad things you've done, your accomplishments, that type of thing."

"So, overall, did I lead a good life?"

"Well … this is gonna be difficult because it's very close. Yes, you have done some good things, a lot of good things, but you've also done some bad things."

"I've not done anything bad", I said, sticking up for myself at that almost shocking accusation. "That's defamation of character."

Michael again twisted up his face then seemed to hesitate slightly before deciding to speak again.

"Well, yes you have. Okay, not really evil stuff like murder or anything, granted, but you have been careless with people's hearts, you know, cheating on girlfriends, picking on kids at school."

"But most people do stuff like that", I said in my own defence.

"Ah, yes exactly. It doesn't mean that its right

though, does it? You know hearts are fragile things, people's feelings do mean a lot. I mean, just because you can't see something doesn't mean that it's no more fragile than a porcelain vase. When people fall in love they give you their heart. Now if someone lent you a book for a while to read, they would expect it to be treated well and returned in one piece without pages missing and a broken spine."

"I take care with items of value."

"When someone gives you their heart they expect you to handle it with care as well. Surely someone's love is worth more than an item of value or something tangible?"

"That does make sense", I nodded in agreement.

"And of course there's pride, avarice, gluttony, lust, sloth, envy and anger. So when you add all of these up it's pretty bad. But of course there are the good things you have done, like helping charities, saving a girl's life, changing people's lives in a positive way."

"But how about other things like... like..." my mind started racing through memories, images flashing by as if they were drawings upon pages of a book. "I've never been racist, I've never been sexist."

"It's not decided like that, it's about the things you have done, not haven't done. You don't win 'Who Wants To Be a Millionaire' by not answering any questions, do you?"

"Well, no."

"It's the same type of thing, you would get minus points if you did, but you don't get any plus points for not, I'm afraid."

Peter came rushing back into the room with a black suit jacket and handed it over. I unfolded it and wore it over my clothing so that the shirt underneath could not be seen and cause offence.

"There you go, perfect fit I'll think you'll find", Peter said, smiling at me like a proud parent seeing their son wear a suit for the first time.

"Thank you … Peter, isn't it?" I asked to make sure I hadn't got his name wrong, I was usually very observant of people and my surroundings but there had been so much to take in since I walked in through the doors, my head was spinning.

"Yes, it is."

"Saint Peter?"

"Erm, yes, you've heard of me then?" he pointed to himself, smiling slightly.

"Well … yes, hasn't everyone?"

"Well yes, they used to, but now we are finding that in the age of Heat magazine readers can name all the previous contestants of Big Brother but not a single Saint or Apostle. Then again, most of them couldn't name the main ingredient of an apple pie. It beggars belief."

"And are you Saint Michael?" I pointed at the man with the shaggy blonde locks.

Michael shook his head and with a laugh in his voice "No, I'm the Archangel Michael, you know, the field commander of God's army."

"Just a question, I don't really want to offend, but I don't really think there's a reason for God to have an army when He's the almighty, or am I wrong?"

"Well you're kinda right. You see, we are all members of God's army, people are his army and that's why I'm manager of Human Resources, same thing when you think about it."

"Fair point, I didn't think of it that way. If I do get

to meet Saint Michael can I take this shirt and get a refund on it then?"

Michael grinned. "Cheeky … you've cheered up all of a sudden."

"Well, I'm still not sure this is real and besides it's not every day I get to meet two famous people, dream or not."

Peter outstretched his hand to shake mine. "Well the sooner you find out if this is a dream or reality the better."

I took Peter's hand and shook it while trying my best to give him a cheery smile.

"Nice to meet you Peter. I hope I get to meet you in the future, a long time after I wake up from this."

"Vincent, I hope I'll get to see you soon and that you settle in okay. I've got to head off now and look after the other new starters. Toodles."

Michael opened the office door leading into the corridor and gestured to me to go first. I wandered through, looking at the painted white brick walls, still feeling slightly apprehensive about what could be waiting for me beyond.

"Laters, dawg", Michael said as he gave a slight wave to Peter then turned to face me. "I hope you are ready because now it's your turn to meet God."

ACCORDING TO GOD

Michael and I walked down a corridor that could have been in any office block. The walls were brick that had been painted the first two feet a dull green, the top half beige. Both colours smacked of the mundane. Double windows allowing light in from the outside were built into these walls about a yard apart from each other. I looked out of the first window we passed, my curiosity was drawn to an office window into a room just off from this corridor, I looked through to see other people working at what I guess were desks. The person closest to the window was a middle-aged, red-haired woman; she was working away, talking to the person opposite whose face was out of my line of sight, although I could see hands moving, gestures within a conversation. I watched for a few moments. Suddenly she looked up as if feeling my gaze. She smiled and waved across to me. I sort of half waved back and carried on walking several steps before we turned off the corridor and walked down another passageway.

"It's okay, we are in a good location here so it won't take us too long to walk to the M.D.'s office",

Michael said, sounding as if he was just trying to make polite conversation, maybe to keep on talking so that I didn't ask any more awkward questions.

"How come we are walking, shouldn't you be flying me there using your wings?"

"No, we don't use our wings up here, well you can see for yourself, look at the size of the corridors and considering the average wingspan of an angel is about six feet. So no, these passageways are really not made for flying about in. But we do use them for convenience on Earth sometimes. The angels that go down there that is, it's just faster, plus anything is better than your transport system. Look at the tube in London for instance, I really don't know how you humans cope with that, it's as hot as hell in the carriages and you always end up with someone's sweaty armpit in your face."

"Not many people enjoy it, I must agree." I recalled the few years I had lived there, standing beside the tube doors minding my own business listening to my mp3 player, feeling a crash into my back and almost being sent flying as someone took a running jump onto the carriage thinking that the doors were about to close. I turned around and pushed him off just as the doors shut, leaving him stranded on the platform. The tube was moving away from the platform as I gave him the 'Vs' through the window.

"Take Saint Paul for example", Michael continued, "He goes down there a lot. He loves his Cathedral, see. He's always harping on about it, no pun intended. He keeps going on about the view from the top being remarkable, he said you can stick your London Eye up your ... well, never mind. Anyway, last time he popped down he got the tube from Euston and had to change at Tottenham Court Road to get the Central line to his stop. He had to wait for five tubes to go by before he finally got on. He's far too much of a gentleman you see, and people just take advantage. They just push and shove and jump on before you. He came back all red-faced and sweaty, so it just goes to show you, it does try the patience of a saint."

We came to a door, which Michael again opened for me to step through first. As soon as I took the first step outside I was almost physically pushed back by the sweetest, natural, most comfortable heat I had ever felt. It was as if this was the first time my skin had felt sunshine. It wasn't uncomfortable, far from it; it seemed to be more than sunshine, it seemed to be radiance, fresh radiance that strangely seemed to perk me up as soon as it touched my skin. The air around me seemed so crisp, so clean.

Various office buildings surrounded us, all different sizes, from long single stories to the office block we walked towards, which was four stories tall. I looked down and noticed underfoot the lush green grass. I then became aware that Michael was not wearing any shoes and I suddenly felt overdressed. "Should I take my shoes off? I'm not damaging the grass or anything am I?"

"No you're fine, player. I never wear any shoes, never have done but you're not doing any harm, so it's fine."

I looked at the buildings around us thinking that it just looked like an ordinary office complex. I didn't say anything to Michael in case I upset him that the place didn't look like anything special.

"Wow, so this is heaven?"

"Erm, sort of, this is the afterlife and we are about to go into Block C."

Again, he opened the door of the building and allowed me to enter first. We then continued up a short flight of four steps and turned the corner to a lift.

"Lift instead of stairs, yeah?" Michael asked as he nodded his head. I smiled, happy at this, as I wasn't in the mood to walk up flights of stairs as I needed to see his boss as soon as possible.

The lift doors slid aside with a 'ding' and we both entered. The grey metal lift could have been any other lift I'd stepped into during my life. Whether it be a department store or office block, they never really differed and neither did this one. It also came complete with two signs, one reading 'max capacity eight people', the other 'Lion of God – lifts', which I took to be the lift creators for the afterlife. I then noticed the sound of Jim Morrison's music being played over the lift's public address system. "A lift in heaven?"

"Yeah, I know it's slothful, but it's a Godsend when you have your hands full with folders and stuff." He put his mouth up to a small speaker in the front of the lift wall: "Floor four please." He smiled back to me. "He's in the top floor, the turret we call it. He's got a lovely office but he does spend most of his time in there, so he deserves some quality."

"So, if I consider myself to be an atheist, how did I end up here? Even though I did have an interest in various aspects of religions it really wasn't for me. I'm more of a creationist."

"Maybe a couple of ways, were you baptised when you were a child?"

"Yes, just after my first birthday my parents had me christened."

"There's your answer then, regardless of what you thought in later life, you officially belonged to our section."

The lift travelled to the top floor and then opened into a typical reception office. There was a glass table piled with magazines arranged in an orderly fashion and soft seats placed around it. A lady was sat behind the main reception desk. She was maybe in her late 40s, but still very attractive, slim with long brown hair tied back into a ponytail. She also wore a crisp white robe. She looked up from the computer she was working at and smiled.

"Good morning Michael, how are things today?" Her voice sounded very professional but caring at the same time. It was the type of voice you could fall asleep listening to... in a good way, not a bad way, I don't mean trying to sleep so you don't have to listen to her ranting like a madwoman. Memories of sharing a bed with some of my ex-girlfriends then came back quickly to haunt me for a few seconds before I dismissed them. However, this woman had a voice you would expect to hear coming from a newsreader, she even looked the part.

"Morning, Mary", Michael replied. "Yeah, not bad thanks. I've just seen Peter, I'm not too sure if he's coming out tonight. When you get a spare minute, give him a ring and try and get him to come out There's karaoke on, he'll kick himself if he misses it."

"Yes okay, I will. How may I help you both today?"

"Just wondering if the chief has a spare five minutes to see us, just regarding Vincent here?" Tilting his head in my direction.

Mary directed her gaze towards me and she smiled. Her large brown eyes then dropped down to look at a large diary that was open upon the desk in front of her. "His schedule is free for a little while, but let me check, just hold on." She picked up the telephone next to the computer and tapped in a number. "Hi, only me. Just wondering if you are free for the moment? I have Michael and a gentleman here to see you. Yes … okay … okay …yes, okay, will do." She put the phone down and then looked back up: "Yes He's free, just go straight in."

I noticed several portrait pictures of people hung upon the wall behind Mary, one of which had a gold frame around it. Ornately carved within the top of the frame were the words 'Angel of the Year'. I looked at the picture of an old gentleman, maybe in his early 70s, grey hair and a kind, smiling face. Underneath his picture was his name: Clarence Odbody. Weird I thought, I'm sure I know that name from somewhere. I continued to look around the room. "I thought there would have been a bathroom next to his office", I proclaimed.

"Why's that?" Mary enquired.

"Oh, I just thought cleanliness was next to Godliness", I said with a wink. She smiled back just as she was interrupted by another call on her phone.

We left Mary to her phone call and walked up to a large set of double doors behind Mary. Michael stopped in front of the door "Oh and whatever you do, don't say that you don't believe in him. He tends to get a little bit tetchy with people who say that."

He knocked on one of the wooden panels, waited a moment and then opened them in front of us. We walked into a large office. The same Jim Morrison music that was playing in the lift could still be heard over the speaker system within the office. I recognised the song as, 'The end'. The office was very plush, circular in shape and, apart from the wall with the door built into it, the rest of the walls were made from glass, looking out onto the buildings and the beauty outside. Within the back of the office was a very old, large wooden desk with only a phone and a filing tray on top of it. Around it were two seats on the visitors' side.

Behind the desk was a large, single, golden chair, with a red leather back and seat, which looked more like a throne than any type of office furniture. Sat upon the grand ornate chair was a slightly portly man with white hair, thick beard and facial hair. I thought that He looked more like the actor Peter Ustinov, or Father Christmas, than God. He was dressed in a golden robe with a red shawl draped over his shoulders, wearing it like a Frenchman wears a jumper. He had five paper forms spread across his desk and was writing things on each one in turn with a quill.

Michael's smile suddenly disappeared and he became serious and professional.

"Morning, sir", he said.

"Ah, Michael, how lovely to see you today, how are things going?" said God, his voice booming across the room in a pleasant but authoritative manner. He was still concentrating on his forms and the task at hand. It was a voice you would expect from a hospital consultant or headmaster.

"Fine sir, thank you for asking."

"Splendid, so who is our guest?" He gestured to the seats in front of the desk. "Please sit down, don't just stand there making the place look untidy."

We both sat down; however, once sat down I noticed that the visitors' seats were made to be a lot lower than God's. Is this so that his visitors always look up to him? I started to feel my annoyance slowly creeping back up again, like a volume display on a television. I wasn't sure if God noticed me thinking and shuffling in my chair, but He cleared his throat and finally looked up from his forms and caught my eye.

"So, what seems to be the problem Michael?"

"Erm ... looks like there could be a slight dilemma sir. This is Vincent, Vincent Dabney", Michael said pointing to me. "...And it looks as though he's come to us too early."

"Oh no, not again. At least it looks like he's taking it well though, hmm, not like John Lennon. I remember that outburst, hmmm, frightful. It's a good job I'm such a big fan of his I can tell you." He let out a loud hearty laugh, which shocked me because I wasn't ready for it. I almost jumped out of my skin, if a soul has skin. I looked down at my hand and pinched myself – ouch; yeah, I definitely felt that, I guess souls can feel. My attention was brought back to the conversation by Michael handing God the manila folder, which He opened and started to speed read.

I cleared my throat, unsure of how to address him or even what to say.

"He said you could tell me how I died?" I asked nervously and pointed to Michael.

God's head snapped up as if shocked to hear me talk.

"Hmmm, what, you don't even know that yet? Damn disgrace; someone should have explained that to you from the get-go. Shall we pick this low-hanging fruit? I'll make a telephone call." He picked up the phone in front of him and tapped in a number.

"Hello, to whom am I speaking? Oh Anita, hello, is Harry about? Yeah, oh is he …" God let out another booming laugh, which would be very contagious if this wasn't such a serious subject we were trying to deal with. "Great, put him on the phone for me will you, thank you."

"Who's Harry?" I leant across and whispered to Michael.

"Ah, you might have heard of him by his other name", He paused and He started to look very sheepish and shifted in his seat as if it suddenly became uncomfortable.

"His other name?"

"Death."

"What? So Death's real name is Harry?"

"Well Death isn't really a name is it? Nice guy, I'll introduce him to you when I get a chance. He's always so busy though, really hard to track him down." I was just about to ask Michael another question about how Death got his name but then God started to speak on the phone again, which stole my attention.

"Harry, yes it's me, are you still giving it 110 percent down there? Good, good, listen old chap, we have a gentleman in the office who seems to have come to us a little bit early … Yes … I wonder if you can tell me how he came over. He's been kept out of the loop on this one so I just need to cascade it down to him ... yes certainly his name, yes his name is..." God flicks back over to the first page of my file "Vincent Dabney ... yes, English ... okay, I'll wait."

God looked over to us and, in a whisper, said: "He's just looking now." He then winked at me. I sat back in my chair, thinking of the situation.

Only moments ago I was enjoying a holiday with my girlfriend and now I am sitting in an office, within the afterlife, talking to the Archangel Michael and God. It didn't seem real, not really how I'd planned the day; in fact it was very surreal and bizarre. Is this the afterlife people hope for back on Earth? Should I be feeling humbled, instead of confused and angry?

"Yes Harry, Hmmm, hmm, yes ... an elephant you say? Really? Ah, yes, that will explain it then. Yes I know, not your fault, just jolly bad luck, what? No, I don't think he's putting a complaint in ... no, a lot calmer than Lennon. Yes, hmmm, okay, I'll let you know. Take care my fellow and I'll speak soon. Okay, good day." God looked at me and smiled as He put the telephone down.

"Well, I'm glad we now have this sorted out. This is what happened: apparently you were feeding an elephant, beautiful majestic creatures I've always thought. Always proud of the elephant, got the idea for testicles when I created them, you know, all that loose hanging skin and trunk ... anyway, I digress.

"It turns out that when your back was turned the elephant wanted more food and as it went for your bag of nuts ... it sort of ... Well ... there's no easy way to say this, but it stuck one of its tusks through your body. You died instantly though, didn't feel a thing, which is always nice for those coming over."

"But how did you not foresee this?", I said, rubbing my forehead, "How was I not expected?".

"It's the animals you see", God said cheerily. A bit too cheerily, I seethed to myself, I've had no sense of remorse or consideration from anyone so far, was it too much to expect?

"The animals? I don't understand."

"I don't control the animals, you see. Oh, I made them but not to be controlled. Man was the being I made in my likeness."

"But didn't you use control to gather them for Noah and his ark?"

"Well… yes… well… no… Well, sort of", said God, his head moving from shoulder to shoulder like a set of scales trying to find a balance.

"What do you mean, sort of?" I held up my hands while I shrugged my shoulders. I really didn't have a clue what He was talking about and was starting not to care.

"Dog whistle."

"Dog whistle?" I echoed at this preposterous answer.

"Yes man, do I have to keep repeating myself?" His voice was turning gruff. "Yes indeed, only dogs can hear a dog whistle you know, well I created one of them but for all of the animals, now that was 360-degree thinking on my part. What, did you think that I made animals like humans, that when they got up here I'd judge them on their lives?

You thought any cat that killed a bird, or leopard that killed a gazelle should be judged and be punished for their sins like a human killing another human?"

"I suppose when you put it like that. Anyway what are you going to do to get me back?"

"Back? What, back into your earthly body?" God asked with a quizzical look.

"Yes", I said slowly whilst nodding my head as if I was talking to a very young child.

"Nonsense and poppycock, there's no getting you back old bean." His commanding voice rejected.

"What, none?" Again my voice suddenly rose, I was finding it hard to comprehend what God was telling me, and it seemed like no one wanted to help. This was supposed to be the person that created everything but he can't do one single task. It wasn't as if I was asking for something that I didn't deserve. There had been a mistake, fair enough, but at least we could acknowledge it and correct it. I was now starting to think I was being taken for granted, something that didn't ever sit easy with me whenever it happened on Earth and I wasn't about to start now. Yet again it seemed like I was victim to terrible management, as I seemed to be continuously up against in life.

"Nope, you see, your body is due to be cremated today, so there's no going back", God said in a matter-of-fact tone.

"Hold on, didn't you bring Lazarus back from the dead", I said, now feeling as if I was in a court of law, without a lawyer and having to fight my case just to get the justice I deserved.

"Yes, but he didn't have a three-foot tusk sticking out of his body. After all, you can't turn a tanker around with a speedboat change."

Damn! I silently said to myself, my mind thinking desperately of ideas to help, some evidence that would prove me correct over God so that he'd have to send me back in some shape or form.

"How about sticking me into a body of someone who has just died?"

"You've been watching too many movies. We don't do stuff like that around here, we aren't B Block you know."

"B Block?"

"Yeah the blocks around here are lettered according to their religion. We are in C Block, C for Christianity. B is for Buddhist and all the others of course.", Michael said.

"Yes, so I'm so very sorry to inform you, old chap, that you are going to have to stay up here and take it like a man. We need you to get on board and be a team player. Thing is though, where shall we put you. Now looking at this, I think going forward we…" God started scratching his beard.

Again I was amazed with what I was hearing.

"How do you mean?"

"Well, looking at your file, your life has been good and bad, however, because you've been taken early and didn't complete the file, there is no final tally, but here is the thing…"

"Final tally, what, so are you saying I'm a terrible person? Okay, I might not be whiter than white, and I agree I was a little sod when I was younger but never in a bad way, and can't you see that my life has got progressively better?" I couldn't believe what I was hearing, I was exasperated.

It wasn't like I was evil, I never stole from anyone, I never robbed a shop or a person, I never took a life, it wasn't like I thrust a spear into his son's side.

"No, I'm not saying that you're a bad person and, yes, that is true, I can see that you have done some rather good things in your life, yes. But look at my predicament, I have to get this right, I can't have you doing the wrong job for eternity, but if you just..."

"Job!" I interrupted again.

"Well, yes, jobs, what else would we do all day? It's not all hopscotch and painting you know. I run a tight ship ... Now, if you'd just be silent and let me finish. As I was saying, looking here I..."

"Well, I just thought it would be a future of bliss. You know, walking around the Garden of Eden, feeding zebras and chatting all day, maybe even some harp playing."

God laughed his big booming laugh, filling the room.

"'Fraid not old boy. It sounds all very nice but this place doesn't run itself. Files like this don't write themselves you know. No, they are done by my filing evangelists, as I like to call them. No, no, no, we all have jobs to do. But we do work hard and we do play hard. Now if you'd just let me finish what I need to tell..."

I looked at the man... person... God, sitting the opposite side of the desk, the almighty creator of everything. I didn't feel astounded or overwhelmed or even bewildered like I thought I would. All I could feel was contempt, contempt not just for everything that had been thrown at me in life, but for unhappiness that had been thrown at others around me.

This thing created the heavens and the Earth, He made darkness and light, He made humans and animals, yet it didn't seem to matter to him the way I felt. It was as if there was no love within him.

I thought about all the friends, family and even a couple of partners He had taken from me and I felt raw.

My memory took me back to one cold February night, when I was walking home from work, I received a text message saying that my girlfriend at the time was in intensive care after a seven-hour operation for a brain tumour.

It was snowing and I was listening to a song on my mp3 player at the time, some unknown artist, playing guitar and singing a slow and mournful tune about some lost love. I walked up the hill through the town that night and passed no one. My bare hands buried deep within my jacket pockets unintentionally protecting them against the cold that I never considered during that walk. The snowdrops mixed with the tears that slowly slid down my face. I felt so alone and that was the exact feeling I had now. She never woke up again and neither did my heart, not for a long time, not until I met Jennifer two years later.

I looked at him and his lack of remorse, and I felt angry. I shook my head as I dropped it into my hands.

"This is bullshit, I've heard enough. No, I do not believe any of this, sorry. All this, 'you can't get back into your body' and the Great Lord almighty being so bloody English. Proves this is all a dream."

"What!" God said, raising his voice clearly annoyed by my statement but I was past caring, this was it, enough was enough. I was never bullied, and I was certainly not going to get bullied in a dream or in Heaven or wherever I am.

"Erm, he didn't mean it boss, just a slip of the tongue, you know, it's all a bit of a shock for him", Michael intervened. He turned to me and whispered: "Didn't I tell you He gets jealous and angry easy?"

"Well, yes, but nothing has convinced me this isn't

just a bad dream. I didn't believe you existed before and so far I'm still not convinced. I mean, the afterlife, just a bunch of offices. It's a bit far-fetched really, and all this management speak is total crap, I mean, 'you can't turn a tanker around with a speedboat change', what does that even mean?

"A bad stomach can make your eyes play tricks, and I've eaten a few dodgy things since I began my holiday. You may be some undigested shrimp, a bit of coconut, a slice of chicken. There's more of ghost chilli to you than ghost. This is all rubbish and you're a load of bollocks", I said adamantly, crossing my arms.

"I don't think I care for that rude outburst. Aren't you just slightly over-egging your pudding rather? Now if you'd only hear me out", said God, sounded more and more like a teacher telling off a naughty schoolboy.

"Outburst? I haven't started yet. I feel like the lone voice in the wilderness here." I stood up, looking down on God who was still sitting.

"You know, if you claim to be some manager of Earth then you are doing a pretty piss-poor job; it's dreadful down there, people are horrible, most of them can't be trusted, most of them are out for themselves. They hurt each other, kill each other, you've got the Earth itself turning upon us with global warming. There's rape, disease, famine, racism, sexism, murder, jealousy, greed, war, despair, fear, hurricanes, tidal waves, volcanoes and earthquakes.

"Then to top it off, I come up here and you can't even patch up a mistake someone made. You ask me if I believe all this is real. After all that, what do you think? No, I'll tell you what to think, you can think that I'm not happy with this, and then you can take your heaven or afterlife or whatever you call it and stick it right up your Godly arse 'cos I am out of here."

I saw Michael physically cringe and he whispered out of the side of his mouth: "You shouldn't have said that Vince me old son".

God stood up, now several inches taller, and looked down onto me. "WHAT! How dare you speak to me with that insolence, boy? You come in here thinking that I don't exist. ME, the creator of the world, of the heavens, of animals, of humans, of flowers, of plants, of vegetables, of light, of darkness, of dinosaurs, of water, of Earth, wind and fire!"

"Cool, did you write 'Boogie Wonderland' as well? I love that song", I said, turning my back to him and moving away from the desk. I started walking towards the door and I felt God following after me.

"You have the nerve to come here and belittle me you mere mortal?" His cheeks bulged out and his head shook with anger.

"What are you going to do, smite me? Come at me with great vengeance and furious anger? You can't even put me back into my own body. Call yourself God. You created the Earth in six days and on the seventh you had a headache and probably created your own arrogance. So I'll tell you what, come down from your ivory tower and then we'll chit-chat."

"How dare you speak to me like that? Where I sit you have no right to stand, I am your Lord and Master", God boomed, his eyes blazing with rage.

"Piss off", I swore, not caring about the sacrilege as I shook my head.

Michael moved in between us as if scared we were

going to come to blows.

"Now you've done it", he said, pushing me slowly towards the door and then turned around to face God. "Look, I'm sure that now he's here and can see all your heavenly splendour."

"No, he has to prove himself", God shouted, obviously infuriated and pointing his chunky index finger at me as He returned to his desk.

"No, his fate should be in his own hands. Take him around and give him the tour and he shall be judged. He will meet five angels and saints whom he must prove himself to and in the end be judged by me." He turned his back and returned to his desk. "Now get out of my sight."

"As you decree, Your Almighty, I'll personally see to it. Just one more thing, your warship, I mean worship", Michael said.

"Yes!" God barked, not even looking at us as we opened the door to leave the room.

"To try and prove to Vincent that this is not a dream, I would like to offer to take him back to Earth. We will just be in time for his funeral."

"Anything, just get out", God shouted, his hand gesturing for us to leave just as much as it looked like He was batting away some tiresome fly from his reach, while still not looking in our direction.

"Thank you, Sire", Michael said as he grabbed me by the arm and almost dragged me out of the office, like a mother dragging an unruly child out of a toyshop. "My word, you don't do anything by halves do you?" he said as he closed the doors behind us.

"Your humility is one thing I'll not miss", I shouted through the door, smiling at myself as I shrugged my shoulders at Michael. "Well, I'm fed up with it all and what do I get from him?" I put on a deeper voice trying to mimic God: "Oh sorry, but I can't do anything, bad luck old bean." I laughed half-heartedly. "That's supposed to help? That's the best the Great Lord Almighty can do? Bollocks."

"You said you didn't believe in him, you told him to... you swore at him … to him … God the creator of everything. Dude, why you wanna do something so messed up like that?" Michael said, sounding like he couldn't believe that anyone would even think such a thing, never mind say it.

Michael wouldn't have been so shocked if he had lived on the estate I'd grown up on, where you had to look out for yourself and stand up to be heard. For the first time he didn't have that beaming smile, in fact just the opposite. He looked sad, his eyebrows now sloping down to the sides, his brow furrowed. I felt guilty that I'd caused it but I had to fight my corner.

"Yes, yes we've been through all of that", I said in an offhand manner. I was annoyed that he didn't get half as worried that I'd been taken before my time, yet when I finally lost my built-up temper at someone, it was suddenly a major problem; that it's me that has the issues.

"Yes, but did you stop and think that this is the person that cast his best friend Lucifer out of here because they had a disagreement. He destroyed Sodom and Gomorrah because He didn't like what was going on there and remember he flooded the world because he didn't like what he saw. He is a jealous God, and you should never forget it.

"Where do you think the word 'God-fearing' comes from? He is a nice bloke, yes, he can be kind-hearted and he has some great stories you might get to hear one day. But now you've upset him, it's gonna take some doing to get back into his good books, and I hope you're willing to try", said Michael, trying to get me to see things from his point of view.

"I always thought God was supposed to be good, kind and forgiving."

"Remember the words of Isaiah 5:20: 'Woe to those who call evil good and good evil; who substitute darkness for light and light for darkness; who substitute bitter for sweet and sweet for bitter'."

"Yeah, and...?" I shrugged my shoulders, as if I knew the scriptures off by heart.

"It is the intent of many of those who make such claims to make a good God look evil, to justify their position of rejecting him, his word, or even his existence."

I shook my head in disagreement.

"Well not really, that's not people swapping one for the other, it's humans just being, well, human, making connections with people's actions; saying if X happens then surely Y is true. You know if Peter Sutcliffe murders women then surely he is evil? If the Nazis invade Poland then surely they are immoral? If the band Take That get back into the charts then surely that is a miracle? That's not trying to prove that God is evil or that he doesn't exist, that's just questioning, that's just scientific."

"Yes, but he never made mankind to question him. He's not too big on the whole being questioned thing. It's just better for people if they don't find out the hard way. When Richard Dawkins gets up here he's gonna wish he was just a florist." Michael sighed and his voice softened. "Come on, we'll take you down to

Earth. The sooner you realise this isn't a dream the better. Mary, could we have two HEV12 forms please?"

"Yes, of course, my dear." Mary said as she started to search through a filing cabinet behind her. "I take it things didn't go too well in there?"

"Hmm, bit of an understatement, but I don't think I said anything that bad", I said innocently. I was now calming down, but still upset that I was on my own with this problem. Now feeling slightly forsaken by God and still not being entirely convinced, this was all too crazy to be reality.

"Well, you might be alone in that way of thinking, Vincent. Oh, apart from the foul language, he did say that he never has and still doesn't believe in Him", Michael said, pointing to the double doors we just came from.

"And he got angry, yes?" Mary asked, nodding, looking as though she had already guessed the answer.

I bowed my head and looked at the carpet below my feet: "Yeah".

Mary reached across and put her hand on top of my forearm.

"Don't take it to heart honey, you are not the first to say that and you won't be the last. Think about it from his point of view. He creates everything and everyone gives you all a lovely, beautiful world as your home and from what I hear these days, people just take it for granted. They vandalise it and take no care of it. Then you stop giving him thanks for anything. Most of the time he only hears from people when they want something in their time of need. So put yourself in his shoes, how you would feel in his place?"

"Yeah, you do have a point", I agreed as I looked up at Mary and smiled back at her.

"He is lovely when you get to know him. A big softy really, would do anything for anyone and he really loves humans you know", Mary said, her smile widening. "Now, if I can just get you both to sign these - there and there - and you can have your security pass." She pushed the forms toward us pointing to the places on them to be signed. Then she handed us a round, plastic security pass, with a holographic image of Saint Christopher. Also in bold and black font, the words 'TRAVELLING PASS' were written across it. Michael hung his around his neck and I followed suit.

My eyes opened wide; there could be hope that he is the all-forgiving creator. "So, do you think he'll change his mind about me then?"

Mary looked at me, smiled warmly and placed a hand on the back of my hand. "Oh no, you're pretty stuffed..."

ACCORDING TO SAINT CHRISTOPHER

Michael and I said our goodbyes to Mary and headed back towards the lift. A silence blatantly gaped between us. My mind was desperately thinking of something to say, yet kept getting distracted by the music - which suddenly stopped, and was replaced by Frank Sinatra's '*Pennies from Heaven*'. However, this distraction was then interrupted by the lift coming to a halt on the next floor down. The doors opened to reveal a slim man with shoulder length, brown flowing hair that was looking off into the distance down a corridor, lost within his own thoughts. He then slowly turned and gazed at me with a very intense stare. He was a handsome man with charisma emanating from him. Slowly, he entered the lift. Although I'd never met this man – he'd died a while before I was born - I recognised him.

"Ground floor please, Michael", he said as he smiled at both of us in turn. He turned his attention to me. "I don't think we've had the pleasure."

I put my hand out, which he shook, giving me a smile and a nod.

"Vi... Vi... Vincent", I stuttered, feeling more nervous than I had with God. The doors shut behind him and the lift continued its journey to the lower floors. His face was just as I remembered from his photos and record covers when he was the lead singer of *The Doors*. He must have been in his 20s back then.

"Well, Vi... Vi... Vincent, I'm very pleased to meet you", he replied.

"You sounded great today, Jim", Michael said.

"Amazing, thank you, that's very kind."

The lift doors opened with a ping and Jim stepped out.

"Well, see you both soon. Stay cool", he said, and wandered off down the corridor facing the lift.

I turned towards Michael and said in a whisper "Jim Morrison". Michael just smiled and nodded.

We both exited the lift and headed down the corridor adjacent to the one Jim walked down. We walked through a maze of corridors for a few minutes, so much so I would never be able to find my way back to the lift by my own devices, unless I'd left a trail of breadcrumbs - which got me thinking: what would you leave a trail of within the afterlife? Bread? Glitter? Maybe fairy-dust?

"So, are you looking forward to going down to Earth?" Michael asked. I was relieved he spoke at this point, as my mind was a blank, as if the idle chitchat part of my brain had been removed. I'd never really been one for talking for talking's sake, it was true that the empty can did rattle the most. I had come across people like that in life time and time again, people who can just talk forever and not actually say anything, certainly nothing of interest.

I noticed Michael's perfect-teeth smile and thought to myself that they must have a great dental plan in the afterlife.

I snapped myself back to the question that had just been asked and thought about it for a few moments. I had mixed emotions about this. Yes, I found it exciting that I was going back to Earth, after all, that was... had been my home for the last 30-odd years. But it wasn't like I was going back home to visit people, not like when I'd moved down south and visited my hometown to see my family every couple of months.

I thought about what it would really mean to watch the church service in which I was the man of the moment. It was distressing to say the least. "What, to watch my own funeral, to see my friends and family in tears? In a word... no."

"Yeah, I suppose when you put it like that. But once you do realise that this is your life now and that you can move on then surely that will be cool... won't it?"

"If you say so", I said, my voice sounding woeful.

"Come on mate, cheer up. We aren't that bad up here. Anyway, ready or not, here we are."

We arrived at a gleaming white corridor, with nothing else but a door and a card reader built into the wall beside it.

Michael took hold of his pass from around his neck and motioned me to follow his instructions with it.

"You need to swipe your card near that thing on the side of the door."

We both swiped our cards; the card reader

"beeped" and a little light built into it flashed green.

"Now Vincent, the way this works is we walk through this door and it takes us to wherever the strongest thought is. So if you cleared your mind and thought of the Empire State Building, that's where we would appear. So I want you to think of the church where your service will be taking place... okay?"

"Okay, I've got it."

"Good, now grab my hand."

I grabbed Michael's hand and we walked through the door. Instantaneously we appeared on the other side. We emerged from a tree facing a church.

"Wow, you mean that was it, we're here? That was pretty cool and painless." I looked down at my body expecting to see it shimmering like a Star Trek teleportation.

"Again, another one of the Managing Director's creations. As He says, up there for thinking, down here for smiting", he said, laughing out loud but stopping abruptly when he realised I wasn't sharing the joke, but rather looking around the church grounds and at the mourners standing around all dressed in black, some chatting to the groups of people they were in, others lost in their own thoughts of sorrow.

"Can you see anyone you recognise?"

I didn't recognise anyone around, so I assumed it must have been the funeral either taking place now or later.

"No, I don't. Should we go into the church?"

Michael nodded in agreement and we both made our way across to the church entrance and entered through the door, which was slightly ajar. As soon as we entered, we kept to the back of the church behind all the pews. I looked up and down the rows of people, each pew full with friends, work colleagues, ex-work colleagues, my girlfriend, ex-girlfriends and family. The vicar was giving a reading from the Bible whilst standing at the pulpit next to a coffin with a picture of myself on top. I realised it was the last picture my girlfriend Jennifer had taken of me before I died on holiday, just after I'd asked her to marry me. The memories of those last five minutes with her came flooding back to me: trying to pluck up the courage to ask that beautiful woman I love and wanted to be with forever to marry me.

"Oh yeah, I do now", I whispered to Michael acknowledging that our journey had found its correct destination. "They can't see me can they?"

"NO, DON'T WORRY", Michael shouted at the top of his voice. I panicked, lifted my index finger to my lips to shush him, using the other hand to cover his mouth while looking around, expecting the entire congregation to turn and stare at us in shock. But everyone just carried on totally oblivious to our presence. I turned back to see Michael laughing. "Sorry dude, just wanted to prove the point … Sorry." He apologised again whilst laughing to himself. "I don't think your loved ones could handle seeing you at your own funeral. You could strip off naked and cartwheel down the centre aisle and no one would be any the wiser. Not that I'm saying you should do that. You're already in hot water with the M.D., you don't want to annoy him any further or, even worse, drag me down with you."

"Did you ever do it?" I asked.

"What, strip off in front of a church congregation? You know I think I can safely say I've never."

"No, I mean when you died, did you come back?"

"No. Well I never died you see, I've always been an angel. So no, I can't even imagine what you must be feeling right now in all honesty."

"It's sad, really sad, not just the thought that I'll never see these people again, but the hurt they must be feeling. I'm really gonna miss them."

Silence punctuated our conversation again while I thought about how much I didn't want to leave these people behind. I wanted to still be a part of their lives.

I looked around at the people in attendance. Some I was surprised but glad to see like friends and relatives I'd not seen for years. My friend Simon with a new girlfriend, I really hope he wouldn't screw it up with this one. No sign of my boss though, which was no surprise. Actually, I wonder if I could come back and haunt him for a while, could be a great idea for some payback in the future.

"It's silly, but don't you think there is something about a church that just makes you want to whisper, like a library, just out of respect?" I asked Michael, but his face looked back blankly at me.

"You mean to tell me you've never been into a library?" A shake of his head was his only reply.

"Who's that lady on the sixth row crying her heart out?" Michael pointed to an elderly, slim lady, dressed all in black, the man beside her putting his arm around her shoulders to comfort her.

"Oh, that's my Aunt Sadie; she's like that at every funeral. I come from a really big family and I've been to, on average, two funerals a year since I was 14. I'm 36 now and, do you know, every funeral I've been to she's cried like that. I was thinking about starting a business called Professional Widows and hiring her out to different funerals if you didn't have many people attending."

"You've had a good turnout. A lot of people cared for you Vince", he said, nodding to himself.

"Yeah, they are all good people. Look, there's my girlfriend Jennifer." She looked so beautiful, clothed in a black dress, her blonde hair falling around her face as she bit her top lip trying to fight back the tears slowly escaping from her eyes.

"It must have been terrible for her when I... was... was taken, all alone in a foreign country, not knowing anyone or able to speak the language and communicate with the locals. Then to have to break the news back home to my family and friends. I really miss her, I worry about her. She's lost weight, she always did stop eating when something was bothering her or she was worried about something."

I wished I could take hold of her and hug her, to tell her that it would be okay and that I would always love her. But most of all I wanted to tell her to take care of herself.

"I asked her to marry me, you know."

Michael nodded, only half listening, seeming more occupied with the vicar's words.

"Really?"

"Yes, it was the last thing I asked her. You know, I was never any good at any of the jobs I had. Oh, I wasn't terrible, I just didn't have any normal aptitude towards them, and it was all sheer hard work that got me through. I really don't think there is any shame in that... you know, to say I'm just okay at doing something.

A lot of people these days seem to get by on saying they are better than they actually are. Look at half the art that gets shown these days. I mean, anyone can get a canvas, put a mobile phone on it, then pour a tin of alphabetti spaghetti over it all, then pass it off as a representation of how the mobile phone is destroying the English language, by people using text speak and abbreviations instead of full words. But it takes skill to paint or draw a nice portrait of a snow scene of a hill and cottages in the background. That kind of art is a skill.

I never possessed any of those skills and wouldn't ever try to pass myself off as having them, but I know that loving her was the only thing I was ever really good at."

"Man, the vicar is doing you a good service. It's all about the angels coming down to collect your soul and the Lord being the shepherd and you his flock; and you going back into his fold for his love to all encompass you", he said, talking to more to himself than to me.

"Just shows you how wrong he is. I mean, no one came to collect me, I never had a shepherd looking after me, I just sort of appeared."

"That's because of your circumstances. If we knew you were coming, you would have been met by someone you were close to and had your reception interview, which explains everything you need to know to get you ready for your future in the afterlife."

"I've hardly been welcomed with open arms by God either."

"Well, everything was going swimmingly till you opened your mouth. If you had done your homework when you were on Earth then you would have known what he can be like. He does like to be worshipped. I mean, look at this place", he said as he pointed around the church.

I looked around at all the people that had turned out, lost within their own grief for me, some crying, some looking down at the floor and some staring at the photo of me, all of them solemn.

All I ever wanted to do in life was to make people happy, to make them feel better for knowing me, but here was the moment I was making a church full of people sad just for knowing me.

"Can we go outside please?" I demanded more than asked.

"Yeah... sure, Vince", Michael's voice dropped as he noticed my look of sheer dejection for the grief for myself.

As we both walked out of the church and into the daylight, I pointed down a path, which led to the bottom of the graveyard.

"Can we walk down there to those graves?"

"Yeah, sure", Michael said, his voice sounding concerned, probably wondering where I was going. Maybe he was thinking I might try to escape and then spend the rest of my eternity on Earth hiding from angels, like some criminal on the run. Maybe they'll get Saint Peter (or Saint Columbo, as I might start referring to him) to try and track me down.

We walked for a short distance down the stone path, passing trees and rows of gravestones of different shapes and sizes -- new, old, well kept, some fallen with overgrown grass around them.

We turned left and walked along another short pavement, passing a few wooden benches with nameplates of remembrance of people past. Almost at the end of the row and beside the final bench, we sat facing a line of gravestones.

"I really don't know what to say at a time like this to be honest Vince; I've not ever been in these circumstances myself. I don't mean to sound harsh, I just want to help. I guess I've never felt loss or what it feels like to be somewhere strange. In time you will feel different. Everything that's given you hurt will be forgotten about, anything that causes you pain will be no more.

"I am here for you. I am your guide for what brief time we have together. Anything you need, I'll try my best to do it for you. If you want to sit here for a while then that's fine, take as long as you need", he said as he patted my shoulder. "You know, I've not been down here in a very long time. Apart from coming down with Lennon. John, I mean, not Vladimir Lenin. I've not been down for centuries."

"Why not?"

"Well, after the Bible came out, we thought that the PR was done and we wouldn't need to do it anymore. Oh, we have saints down here to watch and report back but the management don't get involved like they used to." We both went quiet for a while trapped in our own thoughts.

"Are you going to miss it Vince? Earth, I mean?"

"Yeah, I suppose. It's just hard to think that I'll never see things or go places again. There was so much I wanted to do with my life."

I went through it all in my head, all the locations I wanted to visit, places I'd been to and wanted to enjoy again, hobbies I wanted to start, skills I wanted to learn. Even the smallest things I'd kept delaying like learning a new language, reading Homer's *Iliad*, putting some sink clearer down the bathroom plughole.

"Well you know what John Lennon says about life: "Life is something that goes by when you're playing ice hockey."

"Shouldn't that be 'when you are planning other things'?"

"It used to be, but he changed it when he got hooked on playing ice hockey. Dude, he's an amazing player; no one can beat him. He loves wasting his time with something totally useless and time-consuming."

"It's a shame he didn't get to know Paris Hilton then."

"Oi, cheeky", Michael said grinning and nudging me. "It's good to see you smile again. It's a good crowd up there you know. You have come to somewhere nicer. I know the Managing Director is strict but he's not as strict as he was gonna be."

I sat up, unable to contain my surprise.

"WHAT, really?"

"Yeah, have you ever read Psalm 150?"

"Hmmm, not so much."

"Well it goes: 'Praise God in his holy place, etc, etc; praise Him for his mighty deeds, etc, etc'. Then it goes on about 'Praise Him in the sound of the trumpet, praise Him on harp and lyre, praise Him with tambourines and dancing, praise Him with strings and pipe, praise Him with clanging cymbals, praise Him with loud cymbals'.

"Imagine if that was today's day and age it would be, 'Praise Him with lead guitar and bass guitar, praise Him with saxophone and piccolo, praise Him with bagpipes and penny whistle, praise Him with recorder and flute, praise Him with xylophone and glockenspiel, praise Him with your Hammond and your Yamaha.' See what I mean? It could have gotten really out of hand if he had let it. Do they still make Yamaha?"

"I'm not too sure to tell you the truth. I guess it would be praise Him with your organ."

"Best stop there I think, as we are entering the realms of double entendre."

"You see that grave across there?" I totally changed the subject onto the real reason why I had wanted to sit here.

"The one that says Thomas Dabney? Is he a relation?"

"It's my dad; he passed over about 10 years back. Do you think I'll meet him again in the afterlife?"

"Don't see why not, although it is a big place", he said, shrugging.

"Is there anyway to find out?" I enquired.

"Yeah, but it's all privileged information, you know, personal records and all that, and even in the afterlife people have rights. When people come up they are generally met by a loved one to brief them and ease them in gently before they send them to reception where you showed up.

"Up there all the old conflicts are forgotten, so there are no hard feelings about how you didn't get on and all that. I know you didn't have anyone to meet you but I'm sure once your dad finds out you are here he'll be by your side like a bat out of hell. Actually, do you know how incorrect that earthly analogy is?"

But I wasn't listening to what Michael was talking about; I was too deep into my own memories. Thinking about the special memories of my dad, mostly of when I was a kid, of us playing football in the back garden, him teaching me how to play table tennis on the dining room table, teaching me to ride a bike, helping me with my German revision, of him building a shelf above my bed and it falling upon my head eight hours later, at 3am while I was sleeping, or making some homemade food and accidently giving me food poisoning because the bacon he'd used was out of date. And my final memory I had of him was of us having our first beer together in a pub and finally getting to know him as a person rather than as a father and his final words to me: "I'm proud of you".

"He was a great bloke, never had a bad word for anything or anybody. He was kind, caring, thoughtful and could hold a conversation with anyone regardless of class, skin colour or religion."

"He does sound like a good person. From what I've seen today he raised a good kid as well."

"Thank you Michael, you're a saint."

"No I'm not, I'm an archangel", Michael said, politely misinterpreting my words.

"No, I didn't mean that, I meant … oh, never mind." I looked up at the sky, the sky I always took for granted, never really having taken any notice of the clouds or the sky before.

This time I did. I took them all in as if it was the last time I'd ever see them, watching them sail over the sky with such grace, like thick, grey-white ships.

The cloud directly above us caught my eye. It was pure white, like fresh snow; the edge of it resembled a figure of a man standing up with his arms wide open as if to comfort someone. I wondered if that's where I had been, above those clouds, if that is where the afterlife existed.

"Let's head back to the afterlife."

"Are you sure you've seen enough? I know they can't see you, but don't you want to say your goodbyes?" Michael said, still sounding concerned.

I thought about it for a few moments. Most of me wanted to go back and see the people that came to send me off, to tell them that I'm so thankful I knew each and every one of them. However, no one could see me and I would just feel frustrated. "No, it'll just make me sadder than I already am."

"Oh, I didn't mean for this to make you miserable, it's the last thing I wanted."

"Please take me back." I really couldn't take anymore. It was starting to hurt that I was here but not here, knowing that all the people I knew and loved were just a few seconds away but that I couldn't really be with them, that I don't belong here anymore. Yes, life hadn't been so easy for me but it was still life, my life, and I missed it.

Michael put his hand out and I grabbed it as we walked up to a tree. I closed my eyes and walked straight into it, hitting my head on the tree trunk. I opened my eyes while rubbing my head with my free hand to find Michael looking at me strangely.

"Well you're not going to get back like that", Michael grabbed the pass from around his neck and held it out to the tree, a strange shimmering light weakly emitting from the bark.

"Okay, so I forgot. I'm new to this." I showed my pass to the tree and we both walked through and appeared in the afterlife, outside the very same door in the white passageway we exited through.

"There we are. All safe and sound ... well ... sort of", Michael said, grinning at me still rubbing my head. I nodded, looking down at the floor, still not convinced that this was all for the best. It certainly didn't feel that way.

"Please don't feel down. Look, follow me, we have one last place to go to and then I'll take you home. You never know, you might even grow to enjoy it here", he said cheerily, trying to give my morale a boost. I still wasn't sure if he was this way permanently or if he was just trying to jolly me up.

"Yeah, away from my home, my family and friends."

"Player, as they used to say in Sodom and Gomorrah, don't knock it till you've tried it. Anyway something might happen to lift your spirits."

"I doubt it."

We walked back through a maze of corridors and finally came to a set of double doors, which Michael opened both at the same time. They opened out into a lush green field littered with trees. A huge marquee was positioned in front of us along with hoards of people smiling; some I recognised some I did not.

"SURPRISE!" the crowd shouted in unison, all in a cheerful manner.

"Wha ... wha?", I stuttered not knowing what to think, feeling totally confused.

Michael laughed: "It's your welcome party mate. All your family and friends are here. Well, the dead ones, and of course some general warm wishers."

"But no one knows I died, you said. How come they are here?" My mouth was working for itself as my mind was still trying to comprehend the surprise.

"You've got God to thank for that, he put a few messengers out to get everyone here."

"But I thought he was mad at me?"

"Oh yeah, he is but you forget he loves his children, he always has."

"I don't understand."

"What can I say? He moves in mysterious ways baby. Now go and have fun and catch up. When you are ready to leave come and get me. I'll be mingling and maybe on the dance floor moving in a mysterious way myself!" Michael did a little shimmy, laughed and disappeared into the throng.

I got swallowed up into the crowd amongst the people who patted me on the back and shook my hand warmly. Everyone wanted to talk to me and ask me questions about my first impressions of the afterlife and welcoming me to my new home. The crowd then parted slightly and a figure strode forward in front of me, a figure I recognised and had missed every day for years, the figure of my father. We smiled at each other and I rushed forward and threw my arms around him.

Much later that day, evening, night or whatever time period they have in the afterlife, I managed to find Michael sitting at one of the tables.

"Wow, I've had a great night, mate", I shouted over the music playing in the background while sitting down and patting Michael on the shoulder.

"I did tell you, we do have a great time up here. What did you think of the drink?"

"The ambrosia is gorgeous; it's like drinking that tinned, thick milk you used to be able to get when I was a kid."

"I haven't got a clue what you are talking about", Michael laughed as he shook his head. "But yeah, it is nice, it tastes different to everyone but always something they love the taste of."

"Abraham is a great barman, love the name of his pub, 'Bar Mitzvah.' I thought God's rendition of '*I Will Survive*' was really good and quite surreal."

"Yeah, he loves the karaoke", Michael beamed, his wide grin turning into the widest grin I had ever seen him perform.

"This place looks incredible, it feels as though we're attending a function on Earth, the sky is dark, but light inside the marquees as they have all the fairy lights hanging up and switched on."

"Oh, they're not fairy lights they're the Israel lights."

"It's amazing that there are so many people from all different creeds, colours and religions here."

"Well, again that's the fault of you humans reading things into the Bible that weren't true. Every religion is really about showing your fellow man kindness and compassion, regardless of who he is or what he believes in. I really don't understand why or even how it's been twisted to be used to persecute people, make them outcasts or even start wars. Anyone who does that is seriously missing the whole point of what religion is truly about."

"Hey guys, how's it going?" Peter suddenly appeared from the crowd and sat down at the table with us.

"Hey buddy, you made it", Michael said as he shook Peter's hand.

"Yeah, I wanted to see how Vincent's first day was", Peter said as he directed a smile across at me, waiting for me to divulge the details of the day since leaving his office.

"It's been okay; I managed to upset God, but I've had a good night and it's been great seeing old family and friends."

"Nice one, so you've acknowledged that we are in the afterlife then?" Peter asked.

"Yeah, I suppose. It's hard though." I thought that I might as well accept it. It all seemed real, especially the party and meeting up with friends and relatives that had all passed over, some I'd even regrettably forgotten about.

"You'll be fine, honestly. So what's next?" Peter asked.

"I don't know. What did God say again?"

"Well, starting from tomorrow, you are job shadowing different angels and saints and said he is going to test you. I think depending on how you do with these tests may decide where you end up within the afterlife", Michael explained to us both.

"How hard can that be … which angel is first?" I enquired.

Michael took another breath as if preparing himself for another one of my outbursts.

Just then some live music started up behind us, which sounded suspiciously like Einstein singing American Pie.

"Well, tomorrow we start with Lucy, who you might know better as Lucifer... the Devil."

I didn't catch what Michael said over the live music, so I just smiled and nodded. I'm sure he said the Devil, but I was probably wrong.

ACCORDING TO ARCHANGEL LUCIFER

The landscaped garden we walked through was magnificent; above were perfect blue skies. Underfoot was luscious, flat, green grass, which stretched out around to the white stone complexes around us. Behind, there were hedges with leaves of different shades of green. To the left, carefully placed stones lined the bank of a small stream we followed, which had slow, cascading water running through it.

My mind recalled images of the previous evening and all of the wonders that I'd witnessed. Maybe it wasn't so bad in the afterlife but it still didn't stop me from missing my actual life, my family, friends and most of all, Jennifer. On the plus side I don't ever have to write computer code again unless I get dumped into some Angelic I.T. department. God I hope not. Working with nerds was bad enough. Godly nerds would surely be worse.

"I'd like to thank you again for yesterday, you know, looking after me. Coming to the afterlife before my time was a bit of a shock", I said, giving Michael the best friendly grin I could muster.

He beamed back, his perfect white teeth shining at me. They were so sparkly, I'm sure if I looked close enough I could probably see my reflection in them.

"Hey, no problem, just part of the service, dawg. Did you enjoy the party?"

Dawg? Yesterday it was surfer dude, today hip hop rapper. "Yeah, it was great to see some of my family and friends again. Even strangers seemed to be genuinely nice and happy to see me."

"I did try to tell you, it's not too bad up here. We're a nice group. It was a good party actually. Did you see Jesus' Mother Mary Magda sing '*Like A Virgin*'?. She's got a good voice on her. After you left, me, Joseph of Arimathea and John the Baptist started off a poker game."

"Yeah, well ... yesterday was good and bad. The whole dying thing tends to put a bit of a damper on your day I find. Then, finding out that you died before your time is a bit of a shock to the system and knowing that you've annoyed God just by being honest isn't a nice thought. Do you know what he meant by 'I would be judged'?"

"Not really, I've never heard him say that to anyone before. All you have to do is prove yourself by job shadowing and doing well and then you'll be able to get back into his good books. Just think of these shadowing days as the way to pimp your afterlife. You know, the better you do, the better job you might get."

"What, and it's as simple as that?"

"I guess, if you think that's simple! I mean, no annoying any of the saints or angels, always doing the correct thing. You think you can do that?"

"Hell, yeah." I said, which came out more

apathetic than convincing.

"Hmmm", was all he said in reply.

"Just out of interest though, what would happen to me if I don't please and it all goes a bit... well... wrong?"

"I'm not sure Vince, maybe nothing, maybe stay here or purgatory, maybe better or worse. But don't think like that, you should always think positive. Enjoy the good things about this place then let that enjoyment shine from the inside out. Are you ready for today?"

Michael gave me a comforting pat on the shoulder. He was pretty persistent about proving to me that all was pleasant in the afterlife, which was kind of him. However, I wasn't too sure about the places I might end up if things got a little out of hand.

"Yeah, I suppose. Where are we going again?"

"Well, if I told you that one of the people placed here used to have thoughts that were a bit radical at the time, that the people who surrounded him all said what he was doing was right, but the people that thought themselves as the governing body at the time didn't agree to what he was doing and sought out to persecute and kill him?"

"Is it Jesus?" was my answer to his question.

"Erm, no", Michael snapped sharply back at me, looking at me with an expression like he was going back over what he said for me to come to that conclusion. "I was talking about Hitler, and you are going to see Lucifer. In fact, here we are."

We both stood outside of a three-storey building. Small palm trees surrounded by red poppies led the way up the sides of the path to a green, battered-by-time wooden door. Michael opened the door, allowing me to walk through first.

I looked down the corridor, thinking again that it just looked like another ordinary office corridor, deep red carpet upon the floor, the same sickly green and beige walls I'd seen when I first arrived. These though had seen better days.

All the doors were made of wood and had plaques fixed onto them with the door number on them increasing from HE01. As we both started to walk down the passageway, I noticed that none of the rooms had windows to allow you to look through, like I had seen the previous day inside the reception block. I started to wonder what was on the other side.

Was it so graphically horrible that no one was allowed to see the torment that the evil souls had to endure, which Lucifer enforces on them for their heinous crimes?

"What, so God and the Devil are all in the same complex of buildings?"

"Yeah, this is the entire afterlife. The Hindu Block is just across there", Michael pointed off to the left.

"Wow, that's awesome. What's Lucifer like?" I'd always hated the way people used the word 'awesome'. Very seldom was anything ever awe-inspiring. However, finding out that there was an office block that housed the Hindu offices within the afterlife, as well as meeting Satan, were both facts that I think merited the word awesome - perhaps it is even an understatement.

"Well, Lucy was one of the management in C block, then there was an argument with God and ... Well, that was that really, she got put in charge of this block after losing the old job."

"You know, here's one thing I've never been able

to understand. In the afterlife you have separate places for the good people, and the evil people that are just scum and aren't right in the head, but why don't you have anywhere like that on Earth?"

"What, haven't you been to Milton Keynes?"

I considered what Michael had just said, and then my face felt as if it became so visual with acknowledgement it must have looked as if my mind was a cash register and Michael had just pressed the 'sale' button.

"Fair point …That would explain a lot really."

We came to the end of the corridor facing a door which looked like any of the others we had just walked by.

"Well, we're here, and this is where I've got to bail. Just remember to be yourself and you'll be amazing. I'll pop along after you finish and see how you got on, and then we can go to the snowy fields. They're great, it snows all the time but you don't feel cold and it's still slippery but not hard or wet. Now remember, just be you and don't diss her. Laters, baller." He punched me softly on the shoulder and made his way back.

I looked at the closed door in front of me. The plaque read HE11. I took three long breaths to pluck up the courage, and then knocked on the door. A deep voice boomed out, so loud it was as if it didn't come from behind the door but all around me in the corridor.

"Enter, mortal."

I stepped back in shock and looked back up the corridor for Michael and moral support, but the passageway was empty. I took another deep breath and entered the room.

Inside, the room was an ordinary office; near the

back wall was a desk with a lone chair in front of it. Laid out neatly upon the desk were filing trays full of folders and papers, an inkpad and stamp, also a telephone. Sitting behind the desk was a lady with her back to me rummaging through the middle drawer of a filing cabinet.

"Excuse me, miss, I'm looking for..."

My sentence was interrupted by the walls suddenly turning blood red, hot air blasting me in the face and the voice again that roared out from all around the room.

"Sit, mortal scum and worship your Lord of darkness."

Shaken by this (to what used to be my bones), I quickly sat down on the seat in front of the desk. The figure spun around.

"Hello, Vincent", Lucifer said in a middle-class English and rather pleasant voice. She placed a folder held down onto her desk and opened it up.

The walls slowly faded back to their original beige, however the heat was still persistent. I studied the woman in front of me; she was in her mid-thirties, bookish but attractive, slim with shoulder-length black hair tied back into a ponytail and black, trendy rimmed glasses adorning her face. She wore a deep crimson colour robe, which seemed to shimmer different shades of red as she moved.

"Sorry about the entrance, just a little joke, it seems that's what everyone expects and I do love theatre", Lucifer said, with a pleasant gaze.

"But ..." I replied, although nothing more came out. My mouth and my brain were totally lost for words after that entrance.

"Yes, I know who you are. I've read your file, I

know all about you, what you've done on Earth and also infuriating the Great Lord Almighty on your first day. Not a wise move. One word of advice if I may; God is perfect but he sometimes lets his pride get in the way. But hey, who am I to cast aspersions about that? We've all been there."

She opened up the folder picked up the ink stamp from her desk and stamped the front page twice, the large red inky letters of 'Complete' now permanently marking the page in duplicate. She closed the cover and placed it back into the cabinet behind her, rifling through the files to replace it back in its rightful place. "I know you were angry because your life had been taken away. '*Life is exquisite joys and exquisite sorrows*' Oscar Wilde once wrote."

"How …" I spluttered, as I battled to find the words to put together in a coherent sentence. I then shook my head almost feeling like giving up on trying to construct words. I was unable to figure out what you should say when the Devil is sitting right in front of you; especially the Devil who is being so polite and pleasant.

"I know you're here to shadow what I do for a while, please don't fuss, I will look after you", she said coolly, sounding like she was taking this all in her stride, as if this was a natural occurrence; perhaps it was. Still, this was a big deal for me.

"I must also apologise about the heat in here, the air conditioning has broken down yet again and you know I simply cannot get decent maintenance in this place. Then again, I think I'd have gotten used to it after so long. I get cold so easily; I am terrible in the cold. Anyway, let's abandon this room and I will take you on the tour."

Lucifer stood up and walked around the desk; I opened the door, allowing her to exit the room first, and stepped into the corridor as the door closed with a bang. We moved through some corridors lined with several numbered doors, down some stairs and along another passageway.

"You're not what I expected", I said, finally finding my voice.

"What did you expect?" Lucifer asked, smiling at me, which I wasn't ready for as my statement was meant to be rhetorical.

"Well, something like a horned demon, you know, fire and brimstone. And a man, I always thought you were a man... or in male form. Although they did keep calling you Lucy and looking at your robes, I guess the Devil doesn't wear Prada."

"Ha, funny", she grinned at me in a sort of, 'oh, I've never heard that one before; only for the millionth time this week' kind of way.

"May I enquire why you expected a demon?" Lucifer looked at me intensely, her eyes moving around my face almost as if she was trying to read my thoughts before my reply, which made me feel a tad uncomfortable. I tried to think of something to say to smooth things over and for her not to take such offence, but nothing sprang to my mind.

She shook her head: "Everyone thinks that. That's just all negative PR on Earth. You know like people believe Father Christmas is a big fat guy with a white beard and red clothes, but that was just the way one artist portrayed him and the image just stuck. The image they stole to use as the devil on Earth was an amalgamation of several Pagan Gods: Bes, an Egyptian deity who was actually a protector, Pan the

Greek God and a Greek Satyr. It was a way for the Christian church to demonise the Pagan Gods that they were in competition with. I used to be one of the Seraphim, one of the highest choirs of angels. Have you seen the movie *The Godfather?*"

"Yeah."

"Well, I was like Robert Duvall's character, Tom Hagan. I was God's advisor, looking after all the legalities. Pointing out the good and bad things. Then I lost favour with the Great Almighty. It's nice to hear that they still call me Lucy." She smiled: "It's just short for Lucifer, a term of endearment really, but I thought they had stopped calling me that when I left. It's nice to know. Thank you."

"So what happened, if you don't mind me asking?" I said, hoping she wouldn't mind me asking that question. I thought back to the Bible and how much the Devil was angry at his... her... its downfall.

She started to look wistful for a few seconds as she reminisced.

"Not at all. Well, as I said, God gave me the job as advisor; you know to point out potential problems. So... well ... that's what I did. But he kept taking it as a personal attack to his handiwork."

"Like what exactly?"

"Well, take tobacco for one. I said that those leaves do look beautiful but the humans will take them and use them for something stupid and they'll end up hurting themselves with them.

"But he wouldn't listen. He had more faith in you than I did. I had watched how nasty and evil people could be towards each other. But he was too proud. I suppose it's like any father that won't admit that their child is dumb. You humans value possessions and high rank more than a person's spirit and nature."

"Maybe you have a point, to some extent."

"I did manage to talk him out of the cheeseburger trees at least. I told him leave them to their own devices, people will find a way of making them. If there is something bad for them they will find a way to create it and sell it to others. Where there's a will there's a way, I said. Could you imagine how obese people would have gotten with such a thing? It's bad enough now when they have to waddle down to the shops to buy them."

She fell silent for a while, staring down at the floor as we continued to walk the corridor. I thought she might be reliving the memories in her head.

"But then to add insult to injury, not only does he give me a job and then frowns every time I do it, he then expects me to worship humans! I told him that I'd rather worship camels. Of course that went down like Hitler doing his stand-up comedy routine in the Bar Mitzvah."

"Really?"

"Yes, well camels are such glorious creatures, no airs or graces."

"No, Hitler doing a stand up routine."

"Yes, that was a big mistake, that man just won't repent. He's banned from open mic night now. Anyway, I digress. So yes, I refuse to worship humans and that was it. I got kicked out of my job and got stuck with the role of manager of this block. It's not an easy job looking after these souls, the most desolate of human society.

"But it's not like I was the only one that disagreed with his ideas. About a third of the work force was up in arms. The unions got involved and well let's just say it was messy. There were t-shirts, banners and placards with slogans on them, which annoyed him even more."

"How come?"

"Well, some of the placards had our acronym on it."

"Which was?"

"Well, our group was called the Angels Solidarity Society. You see that's what happens when you get angels to come up with ideas; they're total innocents when it comes to the way of the world."

"And I take it that angered the Almighty?"

"Well yes, but it got worse."

"Really?"

"Well one of the placards read: God doesn't like it. Up the A.S.S. That message got taken out of context, was leaked to Earth and people misconstrued it and used it as more ammunition that God didn't like homosexuals, which he in turn said was my fault.

"I did tell his Lordship at the time, perhaps he should have mentioned something in the Bible, but he wouldn't listen. Now still to this day you get people saying "It doesn't mention in the Bible that God likes gays." Madness when you think about it.

"It doesn't mention the French but it doesn't mean that you should hate them. Okay bad example, The Bible doesn't mention Canadians but it doesn't mean people should hate them. I mean, how specific do we have to be about what's good and what's bad? Did we need to write everything down? Yes, doing good deeds for others is good, that's why they are called good deeds. Yes, not calling someone names behind their back is good. No, placing a firework up a cat's bottom is bad. It doesn't really take a scientist to work these things out."

"How about when you were cast out, wasn't there a battle for three days or something?" I said, desperately trying to remember when I was doing religious education lessons in secondary school and now wishing I'd paid more attention.

"Well sort of, not the type of battle you are thinking, nothing violent."

"So what was it?"

"Well … it was sort of … a game", Lucifer said, flashing me a rather embarrassed look.

"A game, what was the game?"

I started to imagine a grand, hi-tech game of chess where the pieces were real and moved just by thought, and duel to the death with each other when about to be taken.

"Erm … Snakes and Ladders", Lucifer said rather sheepishly.

"Snakes and Ladders!"

"Yeah, well … he loves it. But, a word of advice, never play a game involving dice with someone who controls everything in the heavens and the Earth. Of course, hindsight is a wonderful thing.

"Anyway, that sort of sparked off the whole Adam and Eve thing. The talking snake was a bit of an in-joke between us. I just didn't expect the stupidity of them both. I mean, really, listening to a talking snake! A talking snake, for God's sake! I mean, would you listen to the wisdom of a talking dog?

"That is why he told the saints to give humans the idea to invent schools, to teach people knowledge and hopefully with that common sense. But then they invented reality TV and undid all of that good work."

We stopped outside an office door after walking the full length of the corridor.

Lucifer opened the door and a wall of sound hit us with the babble of people chatting.

"Well, this is the first room I want to show you."

We both stepped into the room and looked around at the many people walking around, sitting at desks, pushing trolleys, filing and answering telephones.

"Wow, there's so many people. How come they are all dressed the same?"

"Ah well, good question. Our robes have different colours but the people I have under me are only allowed to wear green robes. This is where all the fraudulent people are."

"What, like people who bear false witness against God?" I asked, again pulling a distant school memory of having to remember the Ten Commandments for a Religious Education test.

"Yes, and a bit more than that, you know, people who have been counterfeiters, people who just plain lie continuously. Robert Maxwell, that guy from Milli Vanilli, people who work in advertising and PR."

"So what's their punishment?"

"They're copywriters."

"Copywriters in the afterlife?" I blurted, sounding surprised.

"Yes, the saints are Watchers on Earth. They take notes about the people they watch, and this lot copy all the notes up in to the correct folders. Like the folder with all your details in it? Well that had to pass through this department's hands to keep up to date", she explained.

"Erm, not wanting to over-step the mark or look

presumptuous but ... is it wise to have people with past experience of fraud working as copywriters ... surely that's why some of them are here in the first place?"

"No, you are quite astute on that Vincent, we did have one incident a few years back", Lucifer admitted, rubbing the back of her neck. "I probably shouldn't tell you this piece of information, as it's not very, well, common knowledge, really."

Lucifer started talking in a hushed voice: "A while back", she paused and then checked around in case anyone close by could possibly hear. "Hitler managed to escape with the help of one of the forgers."

"Surely he couldn't do much harm up here with all the angels and stuff?"

"Well, that's it", she paused while her face contorted, remembering the stress it caused her at the time and how much trouble she got into. "He managed to escape down to Earth and possess a body and he did untold damage."

"Whose?" I asked, astounded by this revelation.

"Well, let's just say a female British Prime Minister. He apparently wanted to wreak havoc on Great Britain out of revenge. Oh, it was terrible. He closed businesses, factories, mines and shipyards. Whole towns and communities went to rack and ruin because of what he caused. Banning the promotion of homosexuality in schools also stopping free school milk for kids."

I nodded in agreement, remembering it well. I was a kid then and I remembered milk one day then none the next or at all after that. I was a little pleased, as it was never a pleasure drinking half frozen milk that had stood outside all morning in the harsh winters or trying to drink chunks of milk when they were placed next to a hot radiator in the summer.

"You know, I'm surprised people on Earth didn't discover earlier how much evil he was spreading. He even met up with some of the most wicked people in the world at the time and still no one caught on! I mean talk about not even seeing the nose in front of your face", Lucifer said in disbelief.

"So, how did you get him back?"

"Erm …" Seemingly lost for words, she started to rub the back of her neck again. "Yes and I'll have to show you the next room. It's quite remarkable", she said, changing the subject, and started to turn away towards the door.

"Hold on, how did you get him back?" I said, not moving from the spot.

"Erm, well … we … sort … of... haven't yet …" She spoke quietly, hesitantly and slowly as if she was a naughty schoolgirl explaining why she's done something wrong.

"So Hitler is still walking around England?"

"Yes but everyone thinks the ex-Prime Minister is just some mad old crow now, so no one listens to her... him, which really annoys him, I can tell you." Lucifer laughed. "Her poor husband only drank because I think he realised but didn't know what to do, so it numbed the pain."

"Can't you send someone down to get him?"

She shook her head.

"We did try the power of a cleric once to do an exorcism, but it seemed like the host body actually put up a fight to keep the evil soul in there. I don't know, some people just don't know what's good for them if you ask me."

"Can't you just kill her off?"

"What, murder? Now that's not very saintly."

"But you are the Devil."

Lucifer looked visibly shocked by my statement, then raised her hands as if to stop me in my tracks.

"Now, don't go and blame me for the man's sins, I'm above all of that. Besides the body hasn't got too long left. Her gravestone will be the most used urinal in England, which is going to be fun to watch. I am a bit worried to tell you the truth."

"How come?"

"Well, he's had a lot of practice down there closing things down when he was in power as the British PM; when he gets back up he might try and close down all of the furnaces! Anyway, enough of my problems. Come on, I'll take you to the next room."

We walked out of the room, the door swinging to a close behind us. We followed the corridor back to the stairs and went down another flight below and headed along another passageway.

"Sorry my mistake, wrong corridor, sorry, down another flight." She stopped and turned around in one motion.

I didn't move but looked around at the thin layer of dust my feet had disturbed while walking the short distance from the stairs.

"This place is all dusty, how come?"

"We shut down this passageway a while back." Lucifer looked around, looking as if she was thinking about the last time she was down here. "It was where we put the people who abused the deadly sin of gluttony. We started getting a lot of Americans in here that really hadn't done any wrong apart from loving the odd burger and chips. We even had a lot of famous people here: Winston Churchill, The Big Bopper, Fats Domino, Chubby Checker, even Elvis. There was some great music in the corridor; we used to have some good party nights. You see, we aren't allowed to go to the good events that the other blocks get invited to, so it was nice to have our own for a while."

"So, what happened? Did they go on diets?" I joked.

"No, Buddha stepped in and said how unfair it was, said it was not very politically correct. Well, you know what the Great Almighty is like when he's got a bee in his bonnet when someone criticises his work. Oh it wasn't pretty. But Buddha got the unions involved, the M.D. backed down and they all got moved across."

She turned around at the door nearest the stairs. "This is the only room on this floor that's in use. We had it created at the beginning of 2012."

I examined the sign upon the door which read "Ball chair and testicle clamp room."

"Who's in there?" I asked.

"Jimmy Saville."

"Fair enough."

We retraced our steps and carried on down another flight into a different corridor. I felt Lucifer looking across at me, knowing that I was in deep thought and about to ask some kind of searching question.

"Go ahead, say what is on your mind."

"You know what you said before about Hitler escaping?" My mind was still forming the question wondering the best way to ask; thinking if there was any way I could formulate a plan to escape and be back beside Jennifer.

"Yes, but please don't tell anyone about that", Lucifer said putting a hand on my forearm.

"No, that's fine; I just wanted to ask if anyone else had done that? You know, gone down to Earth from the afterlife. I know the Buddhists do it in their block, but anyone else?"

"From this side ... no, I don't think so ... well, a few of the management have."

"Really?" I said with some hope.

"Yeah, the big boss of course, he went down as Joseph, you know, Jesus' father the carpenter, and I went down as Nicodemus", Lucifer said matter-of-fact, as if it was common knowledge to everyone.

"Who?"

"Nicodemus ... don't say you haven't heard of him?" she said, her turn to disbelieve what had just been said.

"Actually, no I haven't, don't you mean Desiderius?"

"No, I don't. If you are talking about the classical scholar who prepared the new Latin and Greek language editions of the New Testament, that was Desiderius Erasmus Roterodamus", Lucifer said, showing off her knowledge of world history and the people within it.

"Well, to tell the truth I've heard of Uncle Remus, who was the fictional narrator of a collection of African American stories and songs. I've heard of The Rasmus, the Finnish rock group. I've even heard of the singer Chaka Demus and Hippopotamus, and even a narrow strip of land, bordered on both sides by water, connecting two larger bodies of land which is an Isthmus, but I can honestly say I've never heard of Nicodemus."

She shook her head.

"You ignoramus."

"I might well be but I've still not heard of Nicodemus."

"Good grief, you humans; don't you take an interest in your world history? Nicodemus was mentioned in the Bible three times. The first time he listened to Jesus teaching, that was just me turning up and letting him know his father was a bit concerned about him. The second time I stated the law to the Romans when he was arrested, telling them that it was an unfair trial. The last was preparing the corpse for burial. There was even a gospel, which told of the Harrowing of Hell, just trying to make a last ditch attempt to try and teach people about conducting themselves with moral integrity."

"Hold on, so God sent you down to look after Jesus?"

"Of course, and your point being?" she said, sounding a little annoyed at my question.

"Aren't you the Antichrist?"

"Here we go again", she sighed. "NO. If you read up on this stuff I am actually the bringer of the light, the morning star. It was actually supposed to be my job at the beginning to go down and spread the word, not Jesus, but the boss said that I had too many prejudices against humans so he sent his son instead. Who botched it up if you ask me."

"What do you mean?"

"Well, they are nice enough men, but just look at the lazy lot he took on as disciples. I mean, one informed on him, some of the others fell asleep when he asked them to keep watch for an hour. Most of them don't know their Thomas Aquinas from their elbow, but please don't get me started."

We arrived at an office door halfway down a corridor and both stepped into the next office. Inside the room a handful of people were sitting around a desk playing cards. They were also all wearing green robes but most of them had paint splattered across them.

"So, who do we have in here?" I asked.

"Well, Vincent, what we have here is the place where the heretics are put."

"They don't look they are being tortured for their sins."

"Tricky thing, heresy. You see, it's a theological or religious opinion opposed to the opinion of the Church."

"Yeah, I know what it means but how is that tricky?"

"Well, that is quite a wide set of boundaries. I mean, look at some of the people we have in here, Darwin, Newton, Einstein, da Vinci. These are some of the most intelligent people ever to roam the Earth. Just look at the 1400s for example; you got burned alive if you owned a copy of the Bible, how mad is that!"

"What, really?" I was genuinely surprised by that fact, especially as people just take it for granted these days. 'These days' I wondered, I guess I'm dead now so there is no such thing as 'these days'. Maybe it should be 'in my day', I thought, my brain heading off on its own tangent.

"Yes, but it's been good news for me though in a way. Take for example, that chap playing cards with his back to us. Do you know who that is?"

Lucifer pointed over to a group of five men all sitting around the table. The man in question looked tall, strong and athletic, had long flowing ginger hair that reached his shoulders and a full beard that came down to his chest. I shook my head.

"No, should I?"

"Well, what if I say he was an Italian artist and scholar who had many talents in addition to his painting. He worked on mechanics, though geometry was his main love. He was involved in hydrodynamics, anatomy, mathematics and optics."

"I think I might have an idea, but go on, give me another clue; an easier one."

"An easier one? You humans take no interest in your own history do you? He was born in Vinci, a small town in Italy. His famous art works are *The Last Supper* and the *Mona Lisa*."

"Okay, maybe not so easy next time. Is it Leonardo da Vinci?" I nodded.

"Correct, well done", she said also giving a small clap.

"So, what is he doing down here?"

"Taking a sneaky break by the looks of it, you see he's a painter and decorator up here. Oh, he still does some art every now and again but that's just for this block. It's almost like a punishment. Even though we can't get involved with the fun things within the afterlife, we can hang the beautiful paintings up to remind people around this block of how good they had it on Earth but spoilt it for themselves and others.

"Excuse me Leo, may I have a word please?" Lucifer said as she marched across to the table.

"Yeees", Leonardo said quite haughtily.

"Did you remove your graffiti off that wall?" Lucifer asked.

"Not yet."

"Why not? I did tell you to", Lucifer said, crossing her arms.

"You do ill if you praise, but worse if you censure what you do not understand." Again, Leonardo sounded quite arrogant.

Lucifer wagged her finger at Leonardo.

"Now, you tried that on Earth and where did it get you? Besides, your graffiti is obscene. I know what an easel is and I don't think Michelangelo would like it stuck there, do you? So I want it cleaned up now", she said firmly but calmly. Then she turned her attention to the others around the table.

"Pssst." I heard but paid no attention.

"Pssst." Again it came from somewhere off to my left. I turned to see a thin man with black, greasy-looking hair, clean-shaven and slightly weedy looking standing behind a pigeonhole for letters. He beckoned me over with a long finger. His head was slightly looking around the office equipment he stood behind.

"Excuse me young squire, I couldn't help but notice thou standing there. May I enquire as to if thou art who I assume thee to be?"

I nodded.

"Very well then, may I assume thou to be a Mr Dabney, am I correct?"

I nodded again.

"A man of few words but great authority I

imagine, sir. Let me introduce myself: I am Robert Spring, Esquire. May I enquire if thou have heard of myself? I know that thou have just come from the earthly existence and graced us with thy good presence quite recently."

"No, I've not heard of you, should I have?"

"No, no probably not. I am previous to your time. When I was... down there I... well let's just say I had some workings to do with George Washington, Benjamin Franklin, Horatio Nelson and Thomas 'Stonewall' Jackson. You see I originally hailed from Britain like your kith and kin but then left to discover my fame and fortune across in the American states. If I may be so bold now that we have become so firmly acquainted. I believe that thee have come up here a little... hmmm, before your time shall we say?"

"Yes, you're right, how did you know?" I firmly nodded to him. At last, could this be someone that actually feels for me and understands what I am going through?

"Well, good and bad news travels fast I suppose and let me be one of the people that will offer you my condolences, if I may?"

"You may. You know, no one so far has really cared that I was taken before my time."

Mr Spring looked shocked and let out a gasp. "Well, on behalf of everyone that does care, please accept my most sincere apologies."

"Why, thank you", I smiled.

"It is because of this 'predicament', shall we say, that I may be able to help thee out."

"Really?" I said in an excited manner.

"Why yes, I detest seeing someone such as yourself trapped up here before thy time. This is truly unjustified. If I may be so bold as to say I would like to propose an offer. May I beseech we get thee back down on Earth? Unfortunately, sir, time to get thou back into thy body has perished, but I do have a connection or several. We could get thee a new body and thou could return within an Earth week, how does that sound to thy ears?"

"Wow", I uttered. I would do anything to be back on Earth, but I wouldn't be me, instead I could get put into a better-looking body or someone with a better life. The possibilities were flying around my head. Then I started imagining that perhaps I wouldn't. Perhaps I would be put back into a body of a down and out with no money or prospects, or an infant so I'd have to live my whole life over again or rather someone else's life.

"Hmmm, I'm not too sure", I said.

"Yes, I gather, nay, appreciate thy apprehension in this matter. Believe me sir, I simply desire justice to be done and to see thee happy and receive what thou deserve. I have come to get to know thee and I do not doubt that thou do deserve the finest. Sir, I want to put thou into a body of someone rich and famous, not just wealthy but obscenely rich; so prosperous that thee could have Bill Gates as thy personal trainer."

He popped his head around the corner again, looking in the direction of Lucifer. "Now, unfortunately I must be brief, may I have a response from thee with haste? Remember, I can put right the inadequacy of the unjust souls that put thee here."

This was my wish come true. I would have done anything to get back to Earth, and not just back in my normal body but finally have the life I deserved. I've never been greedy, I always knew I would have to work all of my life, and I was content at that, but I did always wish for a better life.

The word yes was about to burst through my lips when the angry image of God shouting at me as I left his office also entered my mind. "No, he has to prove himself. No, his fate should be in his own hands. Take him around and give him the tour and he shall be tested."

So, this was part of the test. They thought I was going to fall for it and I'd end up down here with the murderers and thieves. Ha, I caught them out. I smiled to myself.

"No thank you Mr Spring, that is a very kind offer but I am going to have to decline."

"But... bu...", he stuttered.

"I told you what he was like, Vincent", Lucifer's voice was directed at me as she walked away from the table towards me. Mr Spring's ears pricked up and he quickly walked around the opposite end of the pigeon hole document holder.

"You know he never finished most things he worked upon. A good kick up the backside is what he needs. He almost invented the helicopter, he almost invented the parachute, he almost invented the bidet, but he wasn't going to call it that."

"What was he going to call it?" I enquired.

Lucifer's eyes widened.

"Believe me you don't want to know; what you do want to know is that he's got a foul mouth on him, that man."

"When you say painter and decorator, do you mean ..."?

"Precisely what I mean Vincent, come on I'll show

you the others."

As we walked out of the room, I turned my head to see Mr Spring appear around the same piece of equipment again, looking at me with puzzlement. Lucifer and I went back up to the ground level and down the corridor to the outside of the office block.

"Wow, you can walk in the light."

"I keep telling you, you humans took it all wrong, all that being banished to the fiery nether regions and me being evil incarnate was all just made up."

"But aren't you supposed to be the greatest evil that ever existed, the Antichrist that will destroy the world?"

"What, so for thousands of years I'm supposed to hold a grudge and want the world destroyed? Why, just so I can say 'I told you so' to my manager? I'm proud, not petty. This is exactly what I mean; it's entirely wrong. You humans just get things so incorrect. Take the whole 666 thing for example; the real number of the beast is actually 616. For 2,000 years the symbol of the Antichrist has been wrong. Even the European court leaves seat 666 free. But a few years back, some 1,700 year old papyrus was recovered by a university professor and he realised that it refers to the oppressor ruler of the time, Emperor Nero."

"Then how come that's not common knowledge?"

"You're asking the wrong person here, I can't be held accountable for what the human race chooses to accept as truth whether it's the truth or not.

"Look at the blatant evil that's walking the Earth and that people just turn a blind eye to: President Karimov of Uzbekistan, the Westborough Baptist Church and let's not forget Simon Cowell. Hey, did you also know that the roulette wheel adds up to 666?"

"No, I didn't."

"See? This trip is fun and educational! What more could you want?" Lucifer smiled at me. "Here we are."

We were standing outside a construction site with builders walking around a platform busily putting bricks in place of a second floor wall.

"So, what's this?"

Lucy laughed.

"You are going to enjoy this, another game. Guess who that hod carrier is." She pointed to a man carrying a hod full of bricks.

"I don't know, Pontius Pilate?" I shrugged.

"Not even close. Okay, clue time. He was born on Christmas day 1642 and died in 1727. He is one of the foremost scientific intellects of all time. In 1666 he observed the fall of an apple in his garden."

"Is it Sir Isaac Newton?"

"Correct, got it in one. Now did you know that at this time Britain was on the point of economic collapse? He introduced milled coins, which prevented the practice of removing a coin's edge and turning clippings into new coins. He went on to frequent brothels and bars in an effort to hunt down counterfeiters. At least that's what his story was when his friends saw him staggering out of those places."

I laughed.

"Do you see that person up there laying the bricks?"

"Yeah."

"That's Charles Darwin. Now did you know when he was a child he was a bit gullible? Once, a friend convinced him that if he went into any shop in Shrewsbury and wore a special hat he could take whatever he wanted for free", Lucifer sniggered.

"And did it work?"

"Well, he did try it in a bakery shop. He took some cakes and headed out the door, but got a shock when the man made a rush for the door. He dropped the cakes and ran away. He also loved insect collecting."

"Insect collecting?"

"Yes, we were a bit wicked to him when John Lennon came up; we told him one of the Beatles was coming to see him. He thought it was one of his insects coming back for revenge. We managed to catch up with him about seven miles away in one of the meadows, he was still going at a good pace."

"So, was God really angry with him for saying that species evolved?"

"No, not at all. Well, they had to really, I mean He did create the Earth and everything in it, but you know yourself that all of the lands changed from where how they started. Look at the United Kingdom; it was two separate land masses that joined together, one from a really cold region and one from a tropical region. So, animals had to evolve because God made the Earth to evolve within itself. What's the use of creating the Earth and not having anything living on it? It would just be a waste of time."

I scratched the top of my head. "Oh I see, sort of."

"So, are you impressed with them and their lives?" Lucifer asked earnestly.

"Of course, very impressed, man owes a lot to these people and what they achieved." By the glint in Lucifer's eye and the way she was smiling at me I couldn't help feeling that it was a loaded question.

"I'm glad you said that, now do you see that woman coming this way?"

"Yeah, the one carrying that mop and bucket?"

"Well, that's Queen Mary I. She's been cleaning one of the other blocks, now watch this", Lucifer said, anticipating what was about to come.

We both watched as the two men on the platform looked at Queen Mary I walking by, they then shouted down to her.

"Come on darling, show us some leg", Sir Isaac Newton shouted.

"Cor, come on you know you want it, love", Darwin continued the barrage of harassment.

I turned to Lucifer open mouthed. "I can't believe they've just done that."

"Yes, amazing. You take two intelligent gentlemen, stick them on a building site and look what happens."

Queen Mary shouted back: "Jog on you mugs."

In total astonishment I grabbed one of Lucifer's arms.

"Aren't you going to stop her from picking up that brick and throwing it at them? No, you're not."

The brick that was thrown just missed the heads of the two historic bricklayers as they ducked out of its way.

Lucifer laughed: "Perhaps that'll teach them a lesson. She was a force to be reckoned with on Earth, never mind up here. As you see Hell hath no fury like a woman pissed off. Come on, let's go, I'm a bit chilly." She turned around and started to walk back towards the office.

As we walked away, shouts from Queen Mary could still be heard: "Come on down 'ere, I'll show you what for."

"Sounds like they are about to find out why she was called Bloody Mary", Lucifer chuckled. I looked at Lucifer starting to blow into her hands for warmth.

"I can't believe you're cold", I said.

"Oh, I am terrible for the cold, it's because I'm so slim. I blame it on never having the need to eat. I once went down to Newcastle upon Tyne one winter and I was freezing but of course the locals were all wearing T-shirts. I had to go and buy a big coat, I couldn't handle it." Lucifer seemed to shiver just thinking about it.

"What, you went down as the devil?"

"Yes, the full monty: horns, red skin, pitchfork, the lot. All the Geordies kept walking by with me wearing a big winter coat and they were shouting: "Satan, you wanker, you soft poof you." It was very intimidating. I was going to go to London but everyone just shambles about like mindless zombies, constantly looking at down at their phones or mp3 players rather than look where they're walking, so they'd never notice me."

"So, how come you went there?"

"I was sent down by the chief, He wanted to see if people were still afraid of the threat of eternal damnation, so He wanted me to show up as what you humans expected as the devil."

"And the verdict?" I asked.

Lucifer shook her head.

"Surprisingly not. I appeared in a church, again all devilled up and all the congregation just ran out screaming."

"Well, that's good isn't it?"

"All apart from one guy in the fourth row. When I

asked him why he wasn't scared of me you know what his reply was? He said he wasn't afraid because he's been married to the Devil's sister for 35 years. I mean, the cheek of it." Lucifer still sounded hurt. We reached the office block.

"Back into the warmth again. Go on, you first", I opened the door keeping it ajar for her to step through. As we returned back into the building and walked up a set of stairs and along a passageway, I started to think about what my reaction would have been if the Devil had appeared to me on Earth. I turned to Lucifer with a quizzical look.

"Surely that's a good thing, I mean, that people aren't afraid?"

"Just the opposite, people aren't even scared of their own demons, never mind a made up one. Humans don't care for themselves anymore let alone each other. They are sinning faster, more often and without any thought or consideration and that is always bad news."

"But as long as they're happy", I said, not even convincing myself with the last sentence but thinking it was good that I could play Devil's advocate, literally.

"You've got it totally wrong Vincent, that's why people are ending up here instead of with God. He never intended people to be careless with themselves, each other or even the planet for that matter. Look at the Ten Commandments or even Jesus' commandment."

"Did Jesus have a commandment?"

"*'Love each other like you would love yourself.'* People don't seem to do it now and if they do then the people around them think that it's something really special or over the top, when it should be the norm. It's all about what's in it for me, me, me and one-upmanship. You know the sad reality about humans?

"If they all lived on the same land mass, spoke the same language, believed in the same religion and were the same colour they would still find something to hate other people for and start wars. There will always be someone wanting something that doesn't belong to them; there will always be someone annoying them for some reason. Humans love to hate, now that is the sad truth about humanity.

"Look at all the times humans celebrate the end of oppression: the Suffragette Movement, the Civil Rights Movement, the Berlin Wall or Apartheid, it's great that you do this but you really shouldn't have to do it. Speaking of which, come into this room."

We walked into another room; people were cleaning trays and filling up glasses with creamy liquid I recognised as the ambrosia drink I'd tasted yesterday.

"Who are these people? I recognise two of them from the party last night."

"They are the servants, butlers and such like."

"So who were they in life?"

"These are the treacherous fraudulent people, you know people who do evil in the name of the Lord? Evil TV evangelists, dodgy priests, all of the Spanish Inquisition, leaders of the Crusades."

"How come they are the servants?"

"Well, in life all of them said they were the servants of the Lord. However, they did it all for themselves and not only that, they did evil in his name and killed the physical body or murdered the trust of the people that were physically, mentally or financially weaker than themselves. So, up here they truly are our servants. Come on, I'll show you the last room."

We exited the room as quickly as we had entered and strolled the corridor yet again.

"So I still don't get that you are as nice as you are. You're the manager of these people but you really don't like them. You are still the Devil, shouldn't you be sacrificing animals and stuff?"

"The irony of it all is that out of everyone in this place it's me that has the greatest torture. I'm the one that has to look after these people, the custodian of sinners. People I don't like, trust or even want to be near. They have the character traits of everything I warned God about."

"I guess I should have some Sympathy for the Devil." I regretted saying this as soon as it left my mouth as I could see she was becoming a little frustrated.

"You see, again, people point the finger at me for nothing. I've not sacrificed so much as a chicken kebab. Where did you read that I sacrifice animals?"

It then struck me like a lightning bolt that I wasn't sure about where these thoughts had really come from. How I actually did make judgements about things based on information I had just picked up from random places instead of knowing the true facts.

"Well when people are caught sacrificing animals they always tend to say it is because they are Satanists."

"Have you read the Satanic Bible?" Lucifer asked looking really serious and slightly upset.

"No", I responded, wishing I'd never asked the question in the first place. I really didn't want to upset

Lucifer at all, but rather just tease her a bit.

"But you're one of the million people that probably think that it's got lots of 'how to do evil' between its pages?"

"I guess so", I said in a hushed, serious tone, feeling as if I was being reprimanded by a teacher.

"Well, that's where you are wrong. It is a very good read, it does preach about obeying rules, because if there weren't any then the world would be in chaos and no one would benefit. But it also has a paragraph about be kind to people if you want to, hate them if you want to, but don't be two-faced about it. So it preaches honesty."

If I was alive I think I would be blushing by now, listening to Lucifer the Devil throw a strop. I certainly didn't expect that this morning.

"However, I am getting away from the point", she said pointing a well-manicured fingernail at me. "The fact is I've never been down to Earth and said these are the gospels according to me, so how would anyone know what I want?" asked Lucifer earnestly, acting as though she might jump down my throat if I said the wrong thing again.

"I guess they wouldn't", I said, feeling like I did yesterday with God - getting told off for my own personal thoughts.

"Exactly, so first off you have people judging something they know nothing about and secondly, I've never had disciples to preach my word like God or like Jesus. So I don't know why people associate me with killing animals."

I was in two minds as to whether I should try and stop her ranting on by just apologising but I wasn't too sure if this would make the situation worse by not letting her finish. If there was anything I'd learnt from past bad relationships, it was to let the woman finish. So I decided to just listen and nod.

"If you read the Bible, God loves animal sacrifices. Let's take Cain and Abel."

I nodded.

"They both gave him gifts. Cain worked the land and offered wheat to God but He didn't want it. Abel, offered an animal sacrifice, which He favoured. Cain got jealous and killed Abel."

I nodded again.

"Then there's the story of Abraham who sacrifices a few animals in return for the Lord giving him children. So, in fact people should be sacrificing animals in the name of God, not me really."

"I take it you are not happy with it then?" I squinted, almost afraid to ask.

Lucifer's voice raised a pitch. I should have just nodded. Damn.

"How would you like it if your name was bandied about every time something evil happens? Or any time someone unstable goes on a rampage they say they did it in your name? And because of what? Is it written in the Scriptures that I look upon people generously if they do that? No, it's just people not taking responsibility for themselves."

I nodded in agreement.

"There does seem to be a growing number of people like that."

"Absolutely, I mean, look at recent incidents. A kid listens to some heavy metal and ends it all. The parents sue the band, saying that their lyrics instructed him to commit suicide. No, if your kid is that gullible to think that these are anything but words in a song, then you're wrong, it's only music, take responsibility for the way you brought your child up.

"A kid goes on a rampage and kills other children in a school because he's a bit angry at the world, straight away fingers are pointed by family and friends at the schools and authorities. No, take some responsibility, teach your child to turn the other cheek. Teach your child not to lash out when something goes wrong.

"Life is full of up and downs and you have to go through both; yes it is tough but that's life, get used to it. Whatever they are going through, there is someone out there going through a lot worse. Teach them that and how precious life is. As for friends and lovers, have some loyalty, look after your friends, and care about people around you."

She went quiet for a while but I could tell by the look on her face she was thinking.

"Oh and don't get me started on some of the people that preach the name of God on Earth", she said shaking her head. "You see them on an afternoon in a lot of town or city centres, usually preaching at the normal people just going about their business, buying food for the weekend.

"You never see them outside the front door of someone who's committed grievous bodily harm, or gangs, or people who actually threaten and make life a misery for others. Oh no, that would be a little too real, a little too scary.

"Or when did you hear of all these people joining together to become a team of valiant heroes doing good? Stopping muggings, busting drug gangs. They seem to be really good at speaking out against minorities or normal people, just not so brave against the real evil in the world."

Her hands started gesturing as she spoke: "You know it took a group of pop stars in the 1980s to try to stop the hunger and disease in Ethiopia?

"An American comedian started an appeal for a woman in Oklahoma and raised over $125,000 because she said she was an atheist while living in the Bible Belt. Yet I never saw the church payout for all her Christian neighbours for their homes. In the state of Tennessee within the early 1960's, another comedian with the help of a doctor and an automobile dealer built a hospital for children called St Jude Children's research hospital, citing that no child should be denied treatment based on race, religion or how much their family could afford. Now I'm not pointing the finger, but it seems to me that there is more good done by people who don't call themselves believers than the so-called good people.

"Doesn't it seem funny that the world's richest organisation is also the one telling people that it's easier for a camel to pass through the eye of a needle then a rich man to get through the gates of Heaven, yet I didn't see the Pope selling any of the Vatican's paintings to donate money for these people to get their homes back.

"It just seems like there are a lot of people saying they're Christians but not really doing anything helpful. It's all apathetic like selling pots of jam or signing petitions! Where's the passion for love, peace and equality? What's wrong with kicking over a few tables like Jesus did with the moneylenders in the temples? Maybe they're scared of offending the burglars and paedophiles. Perhaps if more people stood up for what's right then burglars, paedophiles, rapists, muggers, murders and gangs wouldn't exist. Can you imagine that type of world? Kind of a world you'd want to live in right? The kind of world where you think that good is winning, that people do have good hearts and want to live in a decent society. But, hey, that would take time and effort and some people probably think 'If I help others then how am I going to get to the top? Where do I benefit?'"

"I think I get the message. So what is in this room?" I said, really eager to change the conversation.

"I'll come down from my high horse now. I will say this last thing, read the Bible. It was God who caused the first argument and because of that the first murder and from what I can see on Earth it's never really stopped, yet it's me who they say is evil. Now, this room is full of some of the most evil people in the world", Lucifer put her hand on the door barring me from opening the door.

I joked: "What, people who work in job agencies, estate agents, and lawyers?".

"Oh no, nothing that bad", she said with ice still in her voice from the tirade she had just unleashed. "No, these are the most sadistic cold-hearted killers of all time", Lucifer said pushing the door handle. She took a deep breath then turned towards me.

"Are you ready to look into the face of pure evil?"

I mentally tried to prepare myself to come face to face with pure evil.

Unsure if I would feel utterly repulsed by them and the punishment that they would endure for all eternity. "I suppose so. I guess..." I anticipated what could be on the other side, imagining a pit of endless torture, hideous screams being inflicted by countless demons.

Lucifer opened the door and we both stepped inside. Within the large office there were about 100 people walking around doing many things with files, reading them, inserting things within them, putting them away within filing cabinets and stacking them into trays.

"So let me get this correct. All these people here have committed acts of evil without so much as a blink of an eye; they had no remorse for what they did. And what is their punishment ... filing?" I said sarcastically.

"Oh filing isn't their punishment, it's their job. This is the post room."

"Hold on, so these people do all manner of evil in the world and when they get up here the worst they have to fear is paperwork?" I said unconvinced, my voice slightly louder, making a few of the people in the room look up to see what the commotion was. Looking around I noticed Josef Mengele the SS physician and Saddam Hussein.

"Not really. In the afterlife we teach you how to release your negative emotions, once you are ready to receive your robes, as there is no need for them up here. However, for these souls we give them back their feeling of reason, their feelings of love, feelings of remorse, of pain and suffering much more intensely than they had upon the Earth. They have to live with what they've done for the whole of eternity. Everyone else who goes to the Managing Director's block has no internal pain or mental anguish. All their worries and problems are forgotten about."

"What, they aren't whipped? They don't burn in the fires of Hell?"

"Wow, you humans are really evil when it comes

down to it. No, we feel that living with the knowledge of their own sins is enough. Plus, we make them speak in tongues so they really can't communicate with each other."

"Yes, and…?" I enquired, waiting for Lucifer to convince me that these people were getting the punishment they deserved.

"Well, they can't communicate with each other. Have you ever worked with anyone when you are just so out of sync with him or her, you just can't seem to communicate?" Lucifer asked calmly.

"Yeah, nothing in common, different points of view", I reply, still unconvinced.

"Yes, well imagine working with that day in, day out for eternity. Don't you remember? It makes it a long day! It's like, say your tortoise started talking to you in tortoise language. You can listen with the best will in the world but nothing makes sense."

"Yes, reminds me of time I spent with some of my ex's friends."

"Were they from far-flung countries?"

"Nah, Glasgow. It still doesn't seem to be enough for the suffering they caused on Earth. It's more cream horn than Daryl Van Horne."

"I think mental pain is always a lot worse than physical. Like sitting through an Eastenders omnibus for example, just not as depressing."

"Yeah, but still", I was still unimpressed.

Lucifer crossed her arms.

"You don't think it's enough to feel the sorrow, guilt and remorse for your sins for all eternity?"

I shook my head and crossed my arms. "No, these people spared no remorse on Earth and they should get their comeuppance."

"I'm sorry if those are your feelings. Two wrongs never make a right. What is Hell? *'Hell is oneself, Hell is alone, the other figures in it merely projections. There is nothing to escape from and nothing to escape to. One is always alone.'* wrote *TS Eliot'.*"

"Well, that's not strictly true is it? I mean, Hitler had somewhere to escape to didn't he?"

She sighed: "I hope that one day you will find mercy. Come on let's leave them to it", she sounded dejected. We then walked out of the room and back to the main entrance in silence.

Lucifer turned to me, still looking unhappy with my argument. Plus, I think upsetting her before didn't help either.

"I hope today has been okay for you?"

"Yeah, it has. Is it over?" I asked, surprised and unhappy with myself that I seemed to have upset Lucifer.

"For the time being, yes. I hope that you will take two things with you at least. The first is that life and afterlife should always be about caring and mercy. If there was more of it we wouldn't have wars, we wouldn't have famine, and we wouldn't have people locking themselves in their homes afraid to walk down their own street."

I nodded, knowing deep down that Lucifer was correct.

"And the second...?"

"It is said in the Bible that God will do good and evil, perhaps you can never have one without the other. But there is nothing wrong with standing up for what is good. A wise man once said the kingdom of God is here within you. As you have been judging, you will be judged."

I shook Lucifer's hand.

"You know, I get it now that this place isn't Dante's *Inferno* or a prison. I guess I just came with a lot of preconceptions and I apologise for that. So am I going to end up down here, is that why I've been shown around?"

Lucifer patted me on the shoulder and smiled a very tender smile.

"You're not a bad person Vincent. You don't need those negative thoughts, they just weigh you down. As for coming down here, honestly I don't really know what God has in store for you. I'm the last person He talks to I'm afraid, but I wish you good luck in whatever it is. Vincent, Euripides said: '*When a good man is hurt, all who would be called good must suffer with him*'. Please take care."

"You too Lucifer, and thank you for your time", I said as I stepped outside of the building once more.

Was that another test I'd buggered up I thought to myself and wondered if there was any way to make amends or was it too late? I wasn't evil but I had infuriated God, and thinking about all of the Greek or even biblical stories I'd read, I don't think any mortal ever got away with that.

"Word up, Vince, how was it?" Michael stood waiting for me beside one of the palm trees.

"Yeah it was okay. I can't believe Lucifer is so nice."

"Yeah, she might have one of the hardest jobs in this place but she's still a good soul. I was gutted when she was moved out of our block. She's got a killer backhand at table tennis."

"What, the afterlife has table tennis?"

"Hey, would it be paradise if it didn't?" Michael

grinned. "Anyway next up you're going to hang with Saint Paul, and can you guess the best news?"

"No, what?"

Michael smiled really wide.

"Vince, my bro. You are going back to Earth."

ACCORDING TO SAINT PAUL

The next Afterlife day.

Michael and I slowly walked along the now familiar corridor where the teleportation door, as I called it, was located. Michael as usual, was smiling, his head swaying in time with a song Whitney Houston was singing over the PA system.

"So did you enjoy last night?" Michael asked.

"Yeah, it was amazing, those snowfields were great. Although I'm not too sure that the Archangel Gabriel understood the whole snow angel concept, which I thought he would, with him being an angel."

"What did you think of the snowboarding and skiing?"

"Totally amazing, never tried those activities before. I've always been afraid of pain, but when there is no fear of injury, it's so much more enjoyable, at least for me anyway. Those Australian adrenaline junkies didn't seem to think so though refusing to do it due to the fact that there wasn't any thrill of impending death. You'd think because two of them were killed bungee jumping, one paragliding, two skiing and one eaten by a shark, that they would have learnt their lesson."

"Are you excited to go back down to Earth again?" Michael enquired.

"I'm not too sure really. It's all been a whirlwind since I arrived here. I mean, just last week I was enjoying a lovely holiday before that elephant killed me."

"Two months have passed since that happened."

"Really!" Earth time really did pass a lot quicker than it did up here.

Michael laid a comforting hand upon my shoulder: "Yeah, well Earth time is measured by the Earth revolving around the sun and the Earth revolving around itself. Up here we don't have that. In fact we only have night and day up here because people complained. We never had it in the early days, but the M.D., sorry, God, gave in to general consensus that it would be a good idea. People got used to it on Earth and kinda missed it once they got up here."

I looked at Michael waiting, hoping to be privy to one of the great secrets of the afterlife.

"So, if we don't get our light from the sun how do we get it?"

He shrugged his shoulders. "Even I don't know that. I did ask God once. He said a good magician never reveals his tricks. Speaking of which, here we are at the teleport door again."

We both went through the motions of getting the machine to accept our cards.

"Grab my hand. Oh, and this time let me think of the location. You just clear your mind. Ready?"

We held hands. Michael opened the door and we

walked through, engulfed within a bright white light and suddenly appeared from a tree around the back of Saint Paul's Cathedral. I looked at the slim tree with its upturned branches pointing towards the heavens and stood opposite a beautiful golden statue of a saint holding a papal staff. I looked around for signs of life but there was not a soul in sight. We walked around to the front steps and into the grand, white ornate building, up to the large brown wooden doors.

"So what's he like? Saint Paul I mean?"

"He loves history, architecture..."

"No, not what does he like, what is he like?"

"Oh, my bad. Hmmm, best word to describe him would be...eccentric, he's a nice guy though. Have you been inside here before?"

"Yeah, I think I came once with the school when I was a kid, I'm not sure though."

Michael's voice then changed to a hushed tone. "Whatever you do, don't say that to Paul when you meet him. He's... well, a bit over protective about his cathedral. So if you can't remember if you've been here or not, you'll just upset him. Now I must leave you here. I'll catch you soon though and see how it went."

"Don't worry I won't upset him", I said, and with a wave of my hand gestured that it would be impossible to even contemplate. Michael looked back and raised an eyebrow, then continued his walk back to the tree leaving me outside of the open door. I stepped into the grand old building. There was no sound coming from inside, no one about, the place looked deserted and tranquil. I ambled down the centre of the room, looking around for any sign of life. I reached about half way down, enjoying the peace and quiet churches and cathedrals always seemed to emanate.

Suddenly I caught a glimpse of something from the corner of my eye, some movement just beside one of the pillars off to the left. I darted around the opposite side of the pillar to catch whatever or whoever it was and came face to face with a man who had grey, shoulder-length, unkempt hair and a long straggly beard to match.

He looked as though he was wearing some kind of brown sack, which also seemed too large for him, his hands and feet hidden under the excessive material and little puffs of dust seemed to appear from it when he moved. I thought that it must be a vagrant using the place to sleep rough or steal some of the valuables or maybe even use the cathedral as a giant ornate toilet.

I moved forward, blocking his path.

"I don't think you should be in here mate. Can't you go to a shelter? Come on mate, you can't sleep in here." The vagrant now looked bewildered. "Look mate if I had any money I'd give it to you but I'm sure if you go outside someone will give you the price of a meal and the cost of a place to stay tonight. Oh … God … and I've just realised that I'm still not alive … and if you can see me then I'm probably verbally attacking Saint Paul", I said, grimacing at my outburst towards my next spirit overseer.

"Indeed I am", the man said looking unfazed by my outburst.

My eyes dropped towards the floor.

"I'm sorry", I said soberly, feeling I'd humiliated myself right from the start. I gazed at Paul's brown 'sack' robe, which now on second glance looked more like a monk's habit, although to be fair it did look like it was meant for someone larger than him. I then looked at the contrast to my flip-flops, beige trousers, dark blue shirt and black jacket I was wearing. I started to wonder if they ever got a change of robes even a choice of colours or styles.

Then I realised I would really miss never ever wearing another pair of jeans, trainers or even a suit, everything I used to take for granted about clothes. I used to moan when I worked in the centre of London, having to wear a suit to work every day, but now I'd give my eye teeth to dress up to the nines in a tuxedo.

"I gather you are Vincent, yes?"

I smiled: "Yes, nice to meet you …" I realised that I'd just taken to calling everyone by their first names but this time it didn't seem quite right, I'd always thought of the luminary as Saint Paul, but I thought I'd best ask before I offended him even more. "… What should I call you? Paul, Saint Paul, Mr Paul … erm … Mr Saint? Look, I'm sorry about just then …"

Paul smiled back, laughing it off. "Please, just Paul and it's fine, think nothing of it. I have been told that you not only hold a conversation but you pretty much strangle it. Have you ever been to my cathedral before?"

I did a very fake "AHEM" cough and remembered Michael telling me not to upset Paul. "Erm... no, no I haven't, but it looks lovely, very...". My mind was working overtime trying to think of a glorious word that wouldn't underrate the building and came up with "…grand", hoping that would be enough of a word to impress Paul.

He smiled, looking very pleased with my comment: "Yes, yes it is."

"And very important", I added, thinking that observation would be the icing that would top off the compliment cake.

Paul's face glowed as he looked around. I took this to mean I was to be given a free guided tour.

"Oh extremely, I love the opportunity to show strangers around the cathedral."

I nodded politely.

"There have been four places of worship dedicated to me to have overlooked the city of London since 604AD. Sir Christopher Wren designed this; the one before was destroyed in the Great Fire of London of 1666. Now that was a real shame, shame, a real shame." He said shaking his head. "It's a very important place you know.

"Some of the most momentous events in history have happened here: coronations, marriages, and funerals. Funerals here have included the likes of Lord Nelson, the Duke of Wellington and Winston Churchill. Do you know, of those significant people..." he wandered off as if in a world of his own. His eyes sparkled as he looked around the building, briefly stopping to place his head on his shoulder and starting to rub it back and forth looking as if he was scratching his shoulder with his head in an unconventional way, or vice versa.

He continued: "Now the Duke of Wellington is my favourite buried here. Did you know he was responsible for many things? As well as his military achievements, the dish Beef Wellington was named after him. The Wellington boot was named after him. He also coined the phrase: 'Being born in a stable does not make a man a horse.' A very important man."

He wandered off to a corner of the cathedral. "Here in one of the transepts is a painting by William Holman Hunt, it's called 'The Light of the World'. Do you see the figure of Christ knocking on the door that opens from the inside? People believe that it is supposed to suggest that God can only enter our lives if we invite him."

I was only half-listening to Paul, my mind wandering and thinking about these heroes of England Saint Paul had mentioned. All the influences their lives had upon people, still to this day. But I'll no longer affect anything or anyone in the slightest upon the Earth. Now that was a weird feeling. How do you get your head around something like that; that you will have no influence upon anything in any way, shape or form? "And does it mean that?" I asked.

"No, it's Jesus delivering a take-away."

That sentence ripped me right out of my private daydream; did I just hear him correctly? Did he just say what I thought he said?

"Are you sure about that? I mean, they didn't even have takeaways in those days did they, did th..." I shot a glance at Paul to see if there was any glimmer of sarcasm or glint of a smirk in his face but realised he had walked off extremely quickly, especially for someone whose oversized robe was dragging behind him. I gave the painting a suspicious glance and then hurried off behind the old man.

I looked around at the immense, beautiful place that it was. Jennifer would have loved to have come here. She always did appreciate beautiful, historic places. I was starting to miss her so much now, wishing that I were alive to share special sights and sounds with her again.

"Now, the top part of the cathedral is the apse, that's where the American memorial chapel is, it's very beautiful, very tranquil. Oh, you see this organ; it was installed in 1695 but has been rebuilt several times. It's the third biggest organ in the UK; it has five keyboards and 7,189 pipes."

"I think my mate Pete has the UK's biggest organ and it's been through more pipes than that, if you know what I mean", I winked and nudged Paul in an over-comical way. However, it didn't have the intended effect and he just gawped at me in complete and utter silence, which then lingered into an uncomfortable pause. "Hey, you knew Jesus when he was younger. Did he ever get upset like all teenagers and say to Joseph: 'You're not my real dad'?" The awkward silence continued.

The sound of voices at the entrance of the cathedral broke the silence. A group of people, each wearing orange waterproof jackets with khaki shorts and walking boots came into the cathedral and started to look around. They had cameras tied around their necks, and carried maps and tourist books. The crowd walked around the entrance section of the cathedral looking at various points of interest and reading from their tourist books about the history of London and their current location.

Paul looked toward them and smiled: "Come, it's about time I showed you what I do." He walked towards the group while I followed by his side. "Now Vincent, I'm what you call a Watcher. I observe people and events and then I report back."

"Who do you watch?" I asked.

"Oh, just people. Not the same person all the time, different people, different times."

"I'm just guessing but don't you miss critical parts from people's lives if you are not watching them constantly?"

Without answering my question Paul strolled over to the group of tourists engrossed in their information books, placed his hands upon the shoulders of one of the men, who appeared totally oblivious to what was happening.

Paul went still for a few moments, as he appeared to be listening to something inaudible to everyone else, human or spirit.

"This man is called Henri, he is from Neuilly-sur-Seine, a suburb in France. He thinks England is okay but prefers France, he's not really interested in this cathedral but he's come along to keep his wife happy. Yesterday he tried traditional English fish and chips for the first time and he loved it. Day before that they went to Epsom Downs Racecourse but they got thrown out."

"Why, were they not dressed appropriately, rowdy behaviour?"

"No, they went into the restaurant, pointed out of the window to the horses running and asked if he could have number 15 Red Feather Boy with potatoes."

I laughed. "Really?"

Paul just nodded his serious expression remaining resolute.

"Wow, this whole reading people, it's amazing. So do you speak French?"

"I understand everyone under the sun. So we don't have to watch everyone all the time, we can just catch up on the relevant bits when we need to. You know like when you haven't watched 'Home and Away' for a month, you can watch one episode and know what's happened straight away?" Paul explained.

"That's really cool. Can I do that?" I asked eagerly wanting to try something new.

"That is only the power of us Watchers, Vincent, but I might let you give it a try along the way. Anyway, if you follow me around to this tree, I want to take you to the streets and show you that this is what my time consists of."

I followed Paul outside of the cathedral and around to the back where the graveyard was located and walked up to the tree where Michael and I had first appeared a short time ago.

"You got here from the main site. Remember, just grab my hand and let me do the thinking", Paul ordered me. He reminded me of one of my old teachers. Counting the kids onto the bus on a field trip, in case any of the pupils had absconded and causing merry hell for some poor, innocent shop-keeper who was just used to a quiet village life and not the turmoil and chaos the 'townie kids' would leave in their wake.

We both showed our security passes to the tree and walked into it instantly appearing on London's Chancery Lane across from... "McDonalds", Paul said. I felt Paul's eyes on me, knowing that he hadn't thought of this location.

We stood on this busy road in the heart of London where various shops and offices line both sides and hoards of people go about their daily routines. A redbrick, ornate building towered over us, looking more like a cross between a Gothic church and a university than a set of offices.

I released his hand and raised mine in innocence. "Hey, don't blame me. I wasn't thinking of food if anything I was thinking about Je..."

And then I was startled at the image emerging across the road, an image I wasn't expecting; a woman walked out of the restaurant door carrying a take-away bag of food. She was blonde, slim and petite; she walked with a slightly stooped head, gazing towards the ground, not taking notice of anyone around her. I walked to the edge of the pavement across the road from where she was.

"Jennifer." The name escaped from my lips and I felt the overwhelming urge to run across the busy road through the speeding traffic to reach her, to touch her, to hold her. In my mind I'd only been away from her for what felt like a few days, yet my heart was feeling the full two months.

I felt Paul walk up to my side.

"Who?" he asked.

"Jennifer, my fiancée." I stared down the road, watching the woman I love walking off down the street while I stood motionless wanting, no, needing to follow her. Even if she couldn't see me I'd be in her presence, but I knew that it wouldn't be enough.

"Oh", Paul said, obviously not knowing what to say for the best. I suspected this was an alien subject to him or perhaps he hadn't felt that emotion for so long it had died within him.

"She looked so lost, so unhappy." I looked at him, wishing that he had the power to lay his hands on me and take the ache I was feeling away. "I miss her so much."

Paul patted my shoulder, knowing there was

nothing he could say to console me or make me feel better.

"I know you do, I know you do. By the looks of it she feels the same way. I don't have to lay-on hands to know that her heart feels as though something is missing. Come on, we'll try and take your mind off it. I remember this area, Holburnestrate. I remember when the old Saint Andrew Church was built near here. And do you see that building over there? It's called Staple Inn. It was once where wool was weighed and taxed and goes back to 1585." He pointed over to a building with a few modern shops below, but above was still an old looking Tudor-style house, high with black and white timbers. "Oh look, there's Bobby."

I took it Paul didn't get out that much as this area was now known as Holborn and has been for a very long time. He wandered off to a pigeon standing on the pavement, and got down on all fours beside it.

"Hello Bobby, how are you today?" The pigeon didn't squeak, squawk, caw or whatever noise it's supposed to use to communicate.

"Yes, I'm here with my friend Vincent, you see Vincent across there." He looked up at me and pointed. Not knowing what I should do I waved at them, realising that I was in the centre of London on a busy lunchtime. I looked around to see if anyone was watching this madness, then realised I was dead and, for once, felt relieved because no one could see me with this nutter talking to some birds.

"Well, lovely to see you again Bobby. Give my love to the wife and kids won't you? Goodbye." He got up and walked back beside me.

"A friend of yours?" I asked.

"Nope, never seen him before in my life", Paul said, and slowly meandered down the street, leaving me behind feeling very confused. I caught up to him outside a clothes shop on the corner.

"Well, while we are here I might as well do some work, no time like the present. Yes, no time like the... erm... present. Oh, look, a pretty lady." He laid his hands upon the shoulders of a lady who was looking through a shop window. She was dressed in a smart suit, holding a briefcase-like leather bag over her shoulder.

"Yes, her name is Sarah Deegan. She works for the court service just a bit further down the road. She works far too hard, hasn't been home to Norwich for about two years and feels guilty, yes very, very sad. She's wondering if she should go back home this weekend; also if she should buy her mother a scarf as a gift." He turned to me.

"You see Vincent, there are some nice people out there. I shall show you a little trick we can do as well." He gave a little laugh as he turned his attention back to the lady and concentrated for a few moments; a smile developed on his face, which then seemed to be transferred to Sarah. He then withdrew his hands. Sarah made her way into the shop; seconds later through the glass she appeared with the shop assistant who took the scarf from the display in the window and then disappeared again.

"What did you do?" I said.

"Oh that, we have a little trick as well as reading someone, all Watchers have the power to put thoughts into peoples' minds."

"Really, so would we, they, feel it?"

"You know when you get the feeling at the back of

your mind when you know something is right or wrong? Or when you get a nagging feeling you've forgotten something? Or you walk in to somewhere and it doesn't feel right?" Paul explained.

I nodded: "Yeah."

"Well, that perception is one of the Watchers looking out for you and giving you advice. Now, saints are slightly different; they have influence, which is like gut instinct, but the thought is so strong you actually think that thought is your own. I'll do it again." He walked up to a man who waited at some traffic lights and placed his palms on him. The man was slim, unshaven, wore a leather jacket, combat trousers and trainers.

"Oh dear, oh my, oh no, oh, oh", he quickly tried to concentrate again, but the lights changed and the man walked away severing the connection between them.

"What happened there?"

"That man, he is about to commit a robbery. Oh dear I hope no one gets hurt." He flapped his arms.

"Shouldn't we do something?"

"I did try. The rest is up to him." He shook his head.

"We're not going after him and try to stop him?"

"It's his life, we can't interfere."

"So we're just going to ignore it and do nothing?" I said.

"Sorry Vincent I can't do anything about it!" He said solemnly.

I shook my head. "So explain this to me, in what cases have you used it?" I tried to think back to my life and if I ever had the 'gut instinct' feeling he was explaining. I certainly didn't get one standing next to the elephant before it killed me. Or when I went out with Joanna Hargreaves, who told me she loved me when I was 15, but broke my heart two months later by leaving me for an older boy who didn't go to school (and who used to supplement his unemployment benefit by selling cigarettes to the pupils walking into my comprehensive school).

Paul deliberated for a while, playing with his beard.

"There was Shakespeare. Yes, Shakespeare there was."

"Wow, you met Shakespeare?" I said, really impressed that Paul had influenced someone I really admired.

"Not only met but influenced some of his works. His comedies especially."

"Such as?"

"Well do you know his play *Much Ado About Nothing* that is set in Sicily? Well, he was going to have the setting originally in Sheffield and it was going to be called 'Owt about Nowt'. Thank goodness I managed to discourage him. Then there was *Love's Labour's Lost*."

"Oh yeah, what was that going to be?" I asked, wondering if Paul was really having fun with me like I thought he had with the painting earlier on, or if he was a little unstable.

"It was going to be set in a zoo, and it was going to be about this keeper called Charlie Love who misplaces some of his animals. It was going to be called 'Love's Lemurs Lost'".

"Hmmm", I said sceptically.

"*Wuthering Heights* was originally going to be called Five Marriages and a hell of a lot of funerals before I stepped in."

"Why don't you use it more wisely, to stop muggers and murderers? Like that guy before?"

He scratched his eyelids with both hands, looking a little odd while collecting his thoughts. "We do if we are present. We do try with a lot of people before they do something terrible, but they either don't listen or are too far gone or even out of tune with reality or out of tune with us. If people don't listen then there's nothing we can do, which is what I tried to do to that fellow."

"Well, what if you all try harder, then you could control the bad people and then things would be great for everyone", I voiced, while thinking to myself that I couldn't believe they don't do it already. Surely I'm not the only one who has ever come up with this idea after thousands of years of crime and atrocity.

"Control the bad people!" Paul's head jerked forward, his long shaggy hair falling over his face.

"Well, you know, not all the bad people, just murderers and chavs maybe. Which is a good point; at what point in your life do you wake up and say, yes I want to be a chav? People think they are the backside of society; anti-social; have bad dress sense; they own small, fat, mental dogs and tons of jewellery. Great, sign me up. I really don't understand at what point that happens.

"And I might add, every time the England football teams are in some kind of tournament the flags come out and they have them draped out of their windows and on their cars. If you don't do it they see it as you not getting behind your team and being unpatriotic. Yet it's those types of people who act in the way that make me cringe that I'm English. If you're Brazilian or Italian then you can get away with it because they have passionate natures and cultures. They seem to embrace the beauty in life and enjoy life. Even if their team wins or loses it's the taking part, it's the being there in the moment. But with the British it's all about 'we are better than you and if you disagree we'll get drunk and beat you up'."

"But Vincent, where do we draw the line at what is good and bad? And what exactly do you stop people from doing?"

"I don't know, I thought the Bible was pretty good at that", I retorted.

I saw a lightning strike further off in the distance, followed by a rumble of thunder and wondered if it was coincidence or not.

Paul shook his head: "We're not here to control anyone, that's why our Lord gave you free choice. Yes, in the early days He was rather strict but that's only because He was trying to build strong foundations. Get the foundations right and everything will be stable. A grain of wheat is just a grain of wheat until it is planted in the ground, but many will be born out of it and live."

"Well, I'm just saying that a lot of pain and suffering could be averted", I said obstinately.

"It's never that simple though", Paul said, looking sorrowful. "Look at wars within the world, there have been times that several countries have sent soldiers in because they were worried about people and their futures being held to ransom by an evil dictator. Evil dictators that tortured and murdered not only thousands of their own people but also their own families. Yet people condemn these leaders for trying to stop that."

I nodded in agreement: "Yeah, a lot of people are

against wars. Some people even say that recent wars were about the resources of these countries."

"But couldn't everyone see it was for the greater good? Let me ask you this Vincent, if something is done for the wrong reasons but the final result is good, does it make that person good or bad?"

I shrugged.

Paul pointed a bony finger at me. "Let me ask you this then. For sake of argument let us say that it was just for profit, they got rid of someone that murdered thousands of his own people. Now if you had a son that was being bullied at school would you want to put a stop to it?"

"Yes, of course I would."

"Well it's the same thing just on a bigger scale, but let me show you what happens. If you see a total stranger getting picked on by a bully would you want to stop it or would it not be your problem and you'd just leave it to sort itself out?"

I thought about it for a while: "I'd do something, but a lot of people would just leave it."

"Exactly, and that's what a lot of people did think. It's not happening in our back yard, it's someone else's problem, let someone else deal with it. We don't control people for exactly the same reasons; because if we help someone, another person would see it as being unfair. We are here purely for observational purposes."

"Okay now I understand", I concurred.

"People of the world need to realise that things would be so much better if we all worked together and helped each other. Sadly, at the end of the day, the world has become what it has because of humans, not through the work of angels or saints." Paul stared at me for longer than I was comfortable with. I was unsure if he was waiting for questions or answers from me, so I did what any man would do and turned my attention towards my shoes.

"Please follow me, come, come", he said as he turned and entered the tube station. People flowed by us, pushing against each other, all in a hurry to get somewhere other than here. We walked through an open barrier and proceeded onto the escalator.

"So, could I try it here now, you know, the reading people thing?" I enquired, turning to Paul, who was on the metal step behind me.

He considered my request for a few moments. "Well, I suppose there is no harm and I guess you are here to try these things. I should warn you that if I pass my power through you it will last for about an hour, so please don't go around doing this to people."

I shook my head; nothing could be farther from my mind.

"So, you put your hands gently onto the person in front and I will put my hands onto you and then I can transfer through you."

He placed his hands upon my shoulders and in turn I placed mine onto a gentleman in front of me dressed in a smart business suit, carrying a briefcase and umbrella.

I felt a warm tingle - as if I'd placed my arms into a nice, warm bath - move through the tops of my shoulders through to the tips of my fingers.

"Okay, now just ask questions in your head, like, what is your name?" Paul instructed. "Tell me about the events of work today? What has been your biggest regret this month?"

I started to concentrate, when I heard a slight

commotion above us. I turned my head to see the man that Paul said was going to commit a robbery running down the escalator, pushing people out of the way with a security guard chasing after him.

As they got closer I debated to myself. I could either do nothing and let him get away with it or act and maybe have to tolerate the rage of God, the angels and everyone else in the afterlife. Ah well, what are they going do? Fire me, kill me or worse, make me do admin. Let them do their worst. I concentrated hard on the gentleman I was touching. Just as the thief got close by the gentleman stuck out his umbrella. The thief's legs got tangled up with the umbrella and he tumbled down the rest of the steps. The businessman was shocked that he thought he'd just accidently tripped an innocent member of public.

"Oops, butter feet", I muttered. Paul's hands left my shoulders, as he watched the raider tumble head over heels with the security guard and tube worker in pursuit.

We stepped off the escalator as the security guard reached the unconscious robber lying on his back on the floor. The businessman quickly rushed past the group that had collected at the base of the escalator, he didn't want to get involved.

"Did you instruct the man to do that?" Saint Paul said, expressing his disapproval.

"I did nothing; I was concentrating on getting something from that gentleman", I pointed to the businessman disappearing around the corner in haste and fluster.

"Oh, really and what did you get?"
"That his name was Charlie."
"Charlie?"

"Yes, Charlie... Charl... ing... ton."

"Oh, Charlie Charlington was his name was it?"

"Well, Charles actually. Unusual name isn't it. That's exactly what I thought. I didn't do a thing. I guess it must have been his gut instinct to do that."

"Hmmm", Paul murmured suspiciously.

We reached the platform just as a light appeared within the tunnel. A guard's voice echoed over the PA system: "This is an announcement to let all commuters know that currently there are delays on the Northern, Circle, District, Metropolitan, Bakerloo, Hammersmith & City, Piccadilly, Victoria and Jubilee lines, however we are operating a good service on all other lines."

"Doesn't that only leave the Central line?" I said to Saint Paul, who replied with a shrug. "Nice to know not much changes in London."

We made our way back to Saint Paul's. Bright sunshine engulfed us as we exited the station and walked back through the streets to the cathedral. I started thinking about Jennifer again, following my saintly companion and not looking where I was going, only to find myself accidentally bumping into someone.

"Excuse me", I said, surprised but polite. I looked up to see a wiry man missing one of his two front teeth, a shaven head, various tattoos adorning his arms, wearing a Newcastle United Football Club strip.

The man pushed his face into mine and snarled: "What did you say to me?"

I took a step back. "Excuse me", I repeated, a bit stunned.

"What are you some kind of southern softy like?" The man stepped towards me again.

I took yet another step back: "No", I said with confidence but at the same time hoping there was still room to keep moving backwards.

"What are you looking at then, do you fancy me, like?"

"Uh, what?" I said, trying to think of something to say to calm him down. However, this seemed to further enrage him.

"You don't know who you are talking to, I'll come at you like a whippet out of a sock; I'll bite your nose off to spite your face. I'll leave you for dead and steal your shoes, man", the man said with venom.

"But I didn't..." I stammered.

Suddenly the man started to laugh in a light-hearted way.

Confused by the two extreme behaviours and worried that I didn't know what this man's next reaction would be I looked for Saint Paul who was just standing watching.

"You're okay, Vince mate, I'm just having a laugh, sorry. Nice to meet you bonny lad. Why man, if it's not Paul. How the hell you doing, like?"

"Cuthbert, my old friend, how are things?" Paul said walking towards us. Cuthbert gave him a friendly hug, slightly lifting Paul up off his feet. I stood a little out of the way, trying to work out what was going on.

"It's been a long time", Paul said to Cuthbert mid-hug.

"Well the football season's been mental man."

"And how did Newcastle United do this year?"

"Ahh, don't talk to me about that man. We were hopeless as usual. I was tempted to appear in human form and streak. I know the gaffer won't like it, but I have needs and pride in me team."

"Tell you what, when you come down for the London games let's meet up and we can go together", Paul patted Cuthbert upon the back

"Aye, that'll be canny. Here, I've thought of a canny idea. Why not get the gaffer to give the humans the idea to make it compulsory for dogs to wear hats?"

"How come?" Saint Paul asked, looking confused.

"Well, just think some dogs are quite threatening, they scare little kiddies and people but if they all wore hats they'll never be scary again. Alsatians wearing a fez, Rottweilers wearing sombreros, Bulldogs wearing bowler hats... problem solved; no more of a threat."

"Okay, I see. Very good.", Paul said. "They could also wear different types of ties?"

"Nah, that's madness. But I like my idea. Am gonna pass the idea on to the gaffer to see if He can implement it. So Vince?" Cuthbert turned to my bemused gaze.

Saint Paul walked towards us, "Vincent I'd like you to meet Saint Cuthbert."

"Sorry again about messing with you before like", Cuthbert said as he shook my hand almost loose.

"It's no problem. I take it you are from Newcastle then?"

"Nah, Scotland originally, but spent most of my life around Newcastle like."

"Although it did get a bit dangerous for you at one point", Paul interjected.

"Aye, you're not wrong there", Cuthbert said, scratching his very closely shaven head. "You see, Vincent, it was like this. There was this woman, see, and she reckoned I got her up the stick."

"The what?" Paul asked.

"Sorry, pregnant. Well, I had to leg it before I got chinned, sorry, beaten up by the father, that's her father not Our Father", his apology was aimed in Paul's direction. "Aye, I was a legend in those parts, a bit like Kevin Keegan, but without the dodgy perm. People used to come on a pilgrimage to my coffin. These days I'm mostly remembered because of the schools named after me. Not much of a legacy, but it'll do. Right then Vince, you're coming with me. Paul, we're gonna have to love you and leave you."

Saint Paul walked over to me and shook my hand.

"Good luck Vincent, I'm sure it will all work out. I hope you find the peace you are searching for. Good luck with it all."

"Thank you Paul for showing me around and being so patient with me. I hope to see you again sometime. Sorry for thinking you were a tramp." I liked Saint Paul, although I'm surprised that people did listen to his teachings back when he was still alive, with his little mad moments.

"Oh, that's fine. I'm sure you will see me again someday", he said with a gleam in his eye. He shook hands with Saint Cuthbert and walked off to his cathedral.

Cuthbert turned to me and grinned a toothy grin.

"Right then Vince, I hope you're ready, because this could get a bit frantic."

ACCORDING TO SAINT CUTHBERT

We stood outside Saint Paul's Cathedral on a beautiful sunny day. Several people walked by, unaware that two spirits stood beside them chatting; one dressed in beige trousers, dark-blue shirt and black jacket, the other in a black and white Newcastle United football shirt which hung down to his ankles, becoming his own version of a robe.

"So then, how are you feeling?" Saint Cuthbert asked.

I raised an eyebrow. "Well I've had better times in my life, so other than the whole being dead thing, yeah, I'm tip bloody top."

"Ah... like that then is it? Right then bonny lad, I'll cheer you up. So, what do you wanna do then?" He smiled as he opened his arms, as if to say the world was our oyster.

I scratched my head whilst I thought about it. "I don't know, isn't that up to you? Don't you show me what you do? As a saint I mean?"

"Bollocks, that's boring. If following me around is what you want to do though, then yeah, we can do that. I just do the same kind of thing Paul does.

Although, I'm also the ideas man, I come up with things to help public relations with the people on Earth but we'll get to that later on. Anyway, back to you, I just thought you'd want to do something... I don't know, a bit more exciting like. Now it's a shame it's not a Saturday because we could have gone to the football. Then again, I've heard that you're pretty down at the moment and the way Newcastle is playing that would only make both of us miserable so that wouldn't be good. Trust me, nobody likes an unhappy ghost, you have to keep your spirits up. Eh, do you get it?"

He laughed to himself, looking off into the distance as if he were performing to some invisible audience and looking proud about the joke he'd just made. "Aye, I've still got it me, sexy and funny, I've got it all."

I couldn't help but give a little grin. "What do I have the choice of doing?"

"Well, let's see", he puffed out his cheeks and scrunched his eyes up as he thought.

"Anything you want I suppose, we could go somewhere not many people get to see, like the top of a pyramid, and admire the view, or see the northern lights, or the Playboy Mansion – that's my personal favourite - or, we could have some fun with people. Look, follow me."

I followed Cuthbert back to the tree I'd just stepped from moments before with Saint Paul and we went through the technicalities and entered the heavenly doorway.

We stepped out of a thin tree on a high street shopping area, a street that had been pedestrianised. Men, women, children, teenagers and families all went about their business, in and out of the shops. Two girls collecting for a British heart charity asking anyone who approached if they wanted to make a donation. Further down the opposite way a Big Issue seller was having the same problem collecting his own personal donations.

"'Ere, I'm trying to help the boss come up with some better public relations slogans. You know those slogans you see outside of churches. I'm having a devil of a time coming up with anything though, yesterday I came up with 'The Garden of Eden, have you forgotten how good it is?' and 'Smited – because you deserve it.' What do ye think?"

"Newcastle Upon Tyne", I murmured.
Cuthbert gave me a funny look.

"What, so you've been here before, then?"

"Yeah, I know Newcastle, I was born here", I smiled back.

"Oh aye, so where do ye live now like?"

"I've just... I had just moved back to London, the last few years."

"Well, at least I don't have to take you on a tour of the area then. So, on to business, one of the things we could do is have a bit of fun with the punters, nothing weird like. Just entertainment with people who should know better."

"I don't understand."

"Here", Saint Cuthbert said, "I'll show you." He pointed towards two young men meeting in the street. They looked quite similar; both medium height, slim build and both dressed in smart casual wear.

"Today should be a bank holiday, we should be off work today John, like", the first man said to the other.

"What, with it being Saint George's day, Steve?", the second man asked.

Steve replied: "Aye, you know Saint George, patron saint of England, he was a true Brit, had a fight with a dragon and saved England. A true Brit I tell ya."

Cuthbert nudged and winked at me: "Watch this." He walked over to John and laid his hands upon his shoulders. The man suddenly shuddered as if a cold breeze had just gone up his spine.

"Well man, you do know that Saint George was Turkish don't you?" John said to Steve.

"No, it's Saint George. It's where Geordies get their name from... so he should be patron saint of Geordies as well like."

"I think you mean Saint George, soldier of the Roman Empire. Patron saint of Canada, Catalonia, Ethiopia, Georgia, Greece, Montenegro, Portugal, Serbia and cities that include Istanbul and Moscow. Born third century. The Emperor Galerius wanted George to take part in the persecution of Christians. George said he was Christian and would not take part; he was then tortured and executed."

"But it can't be. It's where Geordies get their name from", Steve disputed.

"I think you'll find that a number of theories exist as to why people from the north-east are referred to as Geordies. One theory is that there was a Jacobite rebellion in 1745 and the people of Newcastle supported King George II, who stood against the Jacobites. Another theory is that while many miners used lamps created by Humphrey Davy the Newcastle miners used lamps created by the local George Stephenson. These lamps were given the name Geordie after their inventor", John corrected him.

Steve looked at John as if he had suddenly grown two heads.

"Erm... okay man, well, have to go and do some work like. We've just done an audit on our computer system and realised that we have an unhealthy backdoor into our business."

"Yeah, just like your mum", the saint attached to his back couldn't stop laughing.

The only retort Steve had was to leave quickly: "See you after." He rushed down the street, walking as fast as he could.

Cuthbert released John, who started scratching his head, wondering where the information had come from.

Cuthbert laughed: "See? We could do some of that. What do you think?"

"Isn't that dangerous?"

"Why, no! Well, not as dangerous as ignorance anyway." He looked at my face that was likely showing all the signs that messing with peoples' minds wasn't my kind of thing.

"How about we have fun with The Ghost Watchers? Come on."

He took off, not leaving me with a decision to make and yet again we sped through the tree. This time we appeared from a tree located outside a beautiful mansion house. A luscious landscaped garden, full of colourful flowers set out in different rows behind us.

We walked across the pebbly pathway to the entrance, and I noticed we were not making any noise when we walked on it, which was a shame because I loved that sound of gravel underfoot. There was always something satisfying about it, something soothing. Almost like popping bubble wrap or having a relaxing drink after a particularly hard day; or taking off your shoes and socks, letting the summer breeze caress your feet after a marathon run.

In fact thinking about it, the times we'd come down from the afterlife I'd never heard any footsteps, never smelt any smells or felt the wind on my face. Just as well they still happen in the afterlife in some way or form otherwise I would miss those little things.

We walked through the entrance into a hallway and straight into an extravagant room; it was thin and long, furnished with red carpet and deep brown wooden panelled walls. Plush red velvet seats with golden frames were positioned along both walls. Above a large fireplace there was a massive arched mirror stretching almost to the ceiling, next to one of the largest paintings I'd seen in my life and undeniably the largest I'd witnessed in my death. In front of us a small team of three people were setting up a camera and sound equipment, while two others were looking along the walls at the various pieces of art on display.

"Where are we now?" I enquired.

"These, Vincent, are The Ghost Watchers." He turned to look at my face, which was devoid of any expression. "What, you've not seen *The Ghost Watchers* on TV? It's the dead's version of nosey neighbours. What's their motto? 'Witness what will happen to you tomorrow, today'. Yeah, I didn't write it so don't blame me. Although I have to admit that young assistant setting up the equipment is pretty fit, I wouldn't mind showing her my ghoulies, if you know what I mean", he said, giving me a wink while rubbing his hands together enthusiastically.

"What do they do?"

"Oh, they go around to *apparently* haunted locations and try to film ghostly action on camera. It's been going for years, I'm surprised you haven't seen it."

"I can't say I've ever taken an interest really", I said, shaking my head. "Do you try to make contact?"

"Whey no, they can't see us. What generally happens is... do you see that woman, the one with the canny arse?"

He pointed towards two people getting closer to us who were not part of the camera crew.

The man looked like your average TV host: all teeth, hair and fake tan. The woman was slim, mid 50s, and wearing a black trouser suit, black turtleneck and a full-length black coat.

"Yeah, she's the medium, what she does is wander around the house during the day and pick up on the vibes of the spirits." He raised his hands and gestured with his fingers to emulate quote marks when he said the word 'spirits'.

"She even sometimes has chats with them. However, come night time, when they have to camp out and get something on camera, they never get a thing, not a squeak."

"What, nothing at all?"

"You get the usual, 'It's getting colder'. They did a bank holiday special once when they went to people's homes, I followed them around for that one. They went into the kitchen and the medium started blowing on about, 'Yeah, I can feel the temperature drop in this area, it's so cold, it's a few degrees colder than the rest of the house'."

"So had they detected your presence?"

"Na it was the fridge. It's what some people call a load of Hokum, but it's what I call bollocks."

"But it's not totally wrong, I mean... We exist!"

"Oh yeah, that's true, I mean these mediums aren't totally useless, you'll find out about that later, but not from me. This whole ghost chasing, getting them on camera is just all rubbish. If we want to communicate with people then you've seen there are ways and means. We only contact the other side for the good of their future and on our terms, not theirs. It's typical of the human race thinking that they're in control of everything around them, but then they just bugger it all up. How many species of animal have they killed off? As for people like this, they are proof that if you say anything with enough conviction, others will believe without question. Deception to make money, could you live with yourself? I know I couldn't."

"You really think that?" I asked.

"Yeah, some people are gullible and will believe anything. Hey, some people thought the fondue set was a good idea."

"No, I don't think this is my kind of scene either. Anyway, do I call you Saint Cuthbert or just Cuthbert?"

"Just Bert will do. So this is not for you then? Oh well... Okay, how about if I take you back to your life and, before you get your hopes up, I mean so you can watch and see what's going on like?"

"Hmmm, I'm not sure; it'll just make me miss life a bit too much."

"Na, you'll be fine bonny lad, trust me." He

smiled his toothy grin, looking as if his tongue was behind prison bars. I agreed reluctantly and we went into the garden and vanished through the fern tree from where we had come.

We jumped out into what I again thought were unfamiliar surroundings, until I got my bearings and looked around. I then realised exactly where we were; this was the graveyard I visited with Michael not so long ago at my own funeral. Not in the same area though, this was a part of the cemetery I'd only seen from a distance. The rich, deep, green grass stretched underfoot reaching out to the hundreds of gravestones in front of us. However, they weren't the only things in front of us. Directly facing us was my family, my mother and two of my three brothers bending over and placing a few flowers on a grave, a grave I knew was my own. I felt a shiver run through my body.

"What's up, someone walking across your grave?" Saint Cuthbert asked with a half grin.

"Hmmm, nice choice of words, in fact as you can see, yes they are. Why did you want to bring me here, to rub it in? Did God tell you to do this out of spite?"

Cuthbert then got distracted by a girl in her mid-twenties, slim, with long brown hair, scrubbing a headstone with some water and a cloth a few rows down from where my family were. "Now, she's a fox. If I was still alive I'd take her hand, I'd lick her palm, and I'd suck her fingers. I tell you, this life lark is wasted upon the living."

"Do you mind?"

"Oh, sorry mate, I forgot where I was. Anyway, as I was saying, speak as you find mate, that's my motto. I know you had your reasons to have an argument with God and that's fine by me. I like you bonny lad, so no, I'm not trying to hurt you. I just thought it might do you some good, seeing them again. Sorry mate."

I sighed. "No, I guess its fine; it's nice to know that they are still thinking of me."

"So were you close to them?"

"No, I wouldn't say close exactly", I said, not taking my eyes off my family. "We were close when I was a kid. Every year we had family holidays at the same holiday camp in Yorkshire. We never had much money but my parents saved up each year so when we were on holiday, during that week, we'd want for nothing. Good memories, some of the best, it was always a happy time."

"You said you weren't close, but you sounded as if you were. What happened to stop you all being close, when did it change?"

"The truth is…", I thought for a while and came up with a blank. "I don't honestly know. It just sort of happened, we stopped talking and we stopped listening to each other. I don't think we ever stopped caring though. I know that I would have done anything for them. It killed me when I had to move away for a job and be apart from them. I couldn't be there for them. I guess I became more distant, I would have driven myself insane beating myself up about it constantly."

"I guess that was hard. If you really didn't care you wouldn't have given it a second thought. I'm sure you'll get your time with them again in the near future and you will be able to show them that you can be there for them again."

What a strange thing to say I thought. Did he know something but wasn't letting on?

"So tell me about your memories, Vince, what do you remember the most?"

"I owed them a lot. We never had much growing up but they made sure we had clothes on our backs, food in our mouths and a roof over our heads. We weren't rich, we didn't own our own house, I didn't have a great education, but I wouldn't change my childhood at all." I walked up to my family, who were now kneeling to the grave, pulling up the weeds that were starting to appear around the plot.

"I know you can't hear me but I have to say this. I know I never told you, any of you, how I felt, ever, but I love you, I have always loved you and I will always love you. I know you are going through a hard time, but peace be with you all." And with that, I turned and walked off back towards the tree, almost disappearing without Saint Cuthbert, until he realised where I was going and what I was doing. He ran after me and at the last moment he managed to touch my shoulder, flashing his pass in mid-stride and we left the graveyard.

This time I knew exactly where I should be and what scene should greet me as we exited the transport door. A tree-lined terraced street, the house in front of us with the familiar red door and the number 48.

This time it was my companion and not me who asked: "Where are we?"

"We, Bert, are at my girlfriend's house, and we couldn't have timed it any better, because here she is." Jennifer's car came around the corner and came to a stop outside of the house. She got out and walked towards the front door, struggling with a couple of heavy shopping bags in each hand. Rummaging through the black bag slung over her shoulder, finally finding her keys, she unlocked the door and entered the house. I told Cuthbert to come with me and we also entered just as the door was closing.

"I've just had a canny idea, how about this for a slogan: 'Obsessed with perfection since year 0,' or '8 out of 10 people say their souls prefer it'? No, you don't like them?" Saint Cuthbert asked but I ignored him as we entered the house, my intentions being somewhat single-minded.

We walked into the familiar hallway, with stairs in front of us, the kitchen at the end of the hall and the living room off to the left. She dumped her shopping in the kitchen, took off her jacket and shoes at the bottom of the stairs and ran upstairs to run a shower as her routine always had been.

"What, so she's your girlfriend like?"

"Yeah, that's her."

"Wow, you done well for yourself there Vincent, bonny lad."

"Thanks for that backhanded compliment. I miss her, I fell for her as soon as I saw her."

I started to think back to when we met; it was on a train. I was coming back to London after visiting my family in Newcastle, and she was coming back from Scotland after visiting one of her friends that she'd met during her time at university. I asked her if the seat next to her was taken and a tingle ran through me as we gave each other a lingering glance. She smiled and said: 'No, please do'. We began a conversation when neither of us could understand the speaker system announcement and continued chatting for the next few hours. I bought her tea and biscuits from the trolley, helped her off the train with her luggage and we carried on talking.

We went for a coffee and chatted about everything, from bones we'd broken to movies we'd seen, psychology and everything else in between. She lived in London and I lived in Northampton at the time. We swapped numbers and started our slightly distance relationship. I moved down to London to be closer to her after 10 months."

My memories then drifted to some of the times we'd shared at the London Eye, Kew Gardens in the snow, the Aquarium on the Southbank, the romantic weekends away in Oxford and shopping in Cambridge, which was our favourite city in England. Going to see classical music concerts by candlelight inside a church and decorating our Christmas tree together. Holidays in Rome and because I only knew how to say 'Yes' and 'Thank you' in Italian she did all the talking, which somehow seemed to give the locals the green light to try and chat her up in front of me.

"I remember when I first realised that I loved her", I spoke my thoughts out loud, not even looking to see if Cuthbert was talking any notice or not. It just felt good to talk about Jennifer, it made me feel closer to her.

"We were in a furniture store, she was looking for a new sofa. We sat down and tested a dark red leather couch and we both noticed a painting of a New York skyline hanging on a wall; we sat on that sofa not talking to each other but feeling so close, my hand placed upon the small of her back and something just seemed to pass between us, a recognition that we were thinking the same thing without even mentioning it. We carried on shopping for the rest of the day. I never mentioned that shop or the painting till weeks later and I was right, we were both thinking the same thing, how beautiful the painting was and how much we would love to go to New York together one day."

We never did though, sadly something I will always regret.

"Hey, she's running a shower, why don't you go up and have a look for old times' sake, you know", Cuthbert winked and whistled at me.

"WHAT? NO!"

"Go on, I won't tell It'll be the last time you see it all, especially like how you left it. Go on, remember the good times mate, have an ogle. I mean, she is your lass, well ex-lass, so you're entitled aren't you man?"

"No, I'm not spying on her, I might miss her but I'm not a pervert."

"You're not seeing anything ya haven't seen before man. I can't tempt you to listen to your urges then?" Cuthbert said, as he started to scratch his belly.

"No, absolutely not."

"Well you won't mind if I go up and have a look see, will you?", he said as he put his foot on the first step.

"Oi, don't you even dare, get back here. You're not going be that guy are you? Nobody wants to see Mr Creepy so don't even think about going up there because I will give you a nipple twist you won't forget." I walked into the living room over to the TV cabinet, where there was a photograph of Jennifer and I standing with our arms around each other. I felt Cuthbert following behind.

"This was taken at a party we went to together."

"You do make a nice couple, I'll admit it. My advice, Vince, is to get it out of your system as soon as possible. You can't keep it on your mind all the time, and it'll only eat you up inside, bonny lad. No, just remember your happy memories and be happy with them."

"You don't understand, Bert. I never had it easy. I worked really hard to improve my life, it was constantly tough and the only thing that kept me going was the thought of a better tomorrow. She was my better tomorrow, and just when I thought everything in my life was starting to go right, positive karma finally coming back to me, I then get taken away from her. I've had to accept that, since coming over to the other side. Now I should just forget her?

"You know what? If I am expected to just forget her you underestimate love and passion, and if you do that then you underestimate the human soul. Because love is so amazing, love makes us laugh, it makes us sing, it makes us dance in front of strangers and even get permanent tattoos, it makes us believe that if we had one final day it would be bearable because it would be spent with that person."

"So was it bearable, your final day I mean?"

I didn't know how to answer that question, so I didn't. I heard Jennifer's footsteps coming down the stairs and stop at the bottom, as she always did after her shower. I walked out to see the familiar sight of her wearing her pink dressing gown, brushing her wet hair while she looked into the mirror within the hallway. She then stopped, her hands fell to her side and started to cry.

"Vince, I wish you were here, I miss you so

much. I looked around the house for something of yours and there wasn't anything. All I have is your photos and the presents you bought me. I wish I still had one of your t-shirts or jumpers to smell you. You have nothing here, but left everything." She looked into the mirror again; I walked up to her and placed my hands upon her shoulders.

"What are you doing Vince? You can't do that!" Cuthbert said, but I continued, ignoring his advice.

"I can do anything I want", I replied. "God never had a hold over me when I was alive and he's damn well not going to now." I turned to concentrate on Jen, hoping that Saint Paul's powers hadn't worn off. "I just came back to say that I love you so much, I miss you and I will never forget you. No matter what happens, nothing will get in my way of my love for you, you will always be my petal." Then, just for a second she hesitated as if she'd just heard something and smiled. I took my hands from her shoulders, turned to Saint Cuthbert and smiled.

"Oh, Vince", he shook his head. "You're not supposed to do that."

We sat on a hill in the middle of the countryside. I gazed out at the fields before me, listening to the nothingness around. I fell back and lay down into the grass – a mirror image of Saint Cuthbert who lay behind me, our heads almost touching. Lost in our thoughts for what seemed like an eternity, I stared up at the darkness creeping over us, and the stars and moon above smiling down.

"So, why trees?" I asked, breaking the silence.

"What, you mean for travel?" he replied.

"Yeah, why did God pick trees, why not just lampposts or zebra crossings or just zebras for that matter?"

"Trees…Well, for one thing, what is the name of a map you use to travel from one place to another?"

I thought for a few moments: "Would that be a route?", I said hesitantly, unsure if it was correct.

"And where do you think they got that name from? Plus, there have always been trees and there will always be trees."

"Fair enough. So this is Purgatory. It's not how I imagined it, I must admit."

"What were ye expecting then bonny lad?"

I went silent again, thinking for a while, trying to remember all the references to Purgatory I'd heard, read in books, watched in movies or seen in graphic images.

"Well, I think I remember that once you've escaped damnation you make it to Purgatory, where you wash off your sins by doing good. I remember something about a mountain on which, when you reach the summit, you'll be illuminated by the Sun of Divine Grace and ascend to the realm of Heaven… I think that was level one?"

Cuthbert nodded: "Hmmm, what else?"

"The other realms; I think Charon ushers you

across a river, and you find yourself within Limbo, a place of sorrow without torment. Great philosophers, authors, kids that aren't baptised, and others unfit to enter the kingdom of heaven. Caesar, Homer, Virgil, Socrates, and Aristotle are supposed to live there. Level three has no light, the wind is pretty strong and the lustful are blown around endlessly by the unforgiving winds. Level four has eternal rain that is cold and heavy. The gluttons are punished here, lying in the filth and putrid water. Or is level four where the wasteful and the materialistic suffer their punishment, which is sharing eternal damnation with others who either wasted life or lived greedily? I can't remember but pretty much all of them sound like any seaside resort in Britain."

Saint Cuthbert laughed. "No, this isn't Dante's *Inferno* mate. This is it, where it's at. Permanent darkness, stillness, quietness and other things that end with 'ness'."

"So, what is it then exactly?"

"Well... it's just this", Saint Cuthbert said looking around. "It's Earth, but in perpetual twilight, as if daytime gets skipped. Oh, and a mass of fields. It's like a cross between that movie *Groundhog Day* and that TV series *The Prisoner*."

"But doesn't it mean that Hell is a much better place, at least there's other people about?"

"No, in Purgatory you're not serving anyone, in fact you don't have a manager. It's basically time to think, to agree to come over to the afterlife and when God agrees that you are ready. Kind of like a spiritual naughty step."

"So, is that who's here, people who haven't come to terms with their death?"

"More like people who won't come to terms with their death, or won't accept the afterlife exists. Even though they've witnessed it with their own eyes. In fact the most famous person here should be turning up any time soon."

"Do you think God will send me here then, if I don't appease him?"

"I honestly don't know, bonny lad. I try not to get involved with it all. It's possible. Do you think you've been a naughty lad then?"

"Let's see, so far I've had a pop at God, annoyed Lucifer, went against Saint Paul's rules, oh and yours. Other than that I'm doing okay."

"Aye well, you are who you are I suppose. Like me when I was a lad, I was a proper love machine me, man." He got up from the grass and started to dance like a robot and moonwalk while singing:

"I like it, I love it, I touch my ass and rub it."

"Hmmm, nice song. Anyway, I always thought that Purgatory would be like Canada, you know the best bits of England and the best bits from America. I thought it would be the best bits of Heaven and Hell."

Saint Cuthbert sat back down in the same spot he was in previously.

"It's a bit of a halfway house between the living and the afterlife, but you can get out anytime you want when you accept everything. Hey, that slogan thing, how about, 'You don't have to believe to be saved, but it helps', or, 'In business for life'? Oh, I know, how about 'Who's the daddy?'. No? I know, 'Join Noah or face Hell and high water'."

I shook my head as they were all terrible ideas.

"Please yourself then. Here's a joke for you

Vince, what time of day did God create Adam?"

"I don't know?"

"A little before eve … eh, do you get it …?"

Again I shook my head.

"Oh, come on, that was funny. Ah well, never mind."

"Is this where suicide victims are put?" I asked.

"Na, poor souls, haven't they had a bad enough life? We wouldn't want to make things just as bad for them up here." Cuthbert deliberated for a while. "Why do you ask, were you going to end it all at some point?"

"Well, when I'm standing at the edge of a cliff I do get an overwhelming feeling to toss myself off but that's a different matter. But no, despite some really low points in life."

Just then our attentions were turned to the sound of lyrics from a song I knew and remembered. It was the group T-Rex, the male voice sang: "You won't fool the children of the revolution". A man walked over towards us, he was quite large with white hair, which seamlessly joined into his full white beard. His big moustache was brown. "Cuthbert, what are you doing here?" the man shouted as he approached us.

"Karl mate, how's tricks?" Cuthbert said, sitting up and swivelling around to face the approaching acquaintance. Without standing he stretched his arm out and the men both greeted each other with a handshake. The stranger sat down on the grass facing us.

"What brings you to these parts?" Karl asked in a faint German accent. "You have not been around for a lot of the time."

"This lad here, I wanted to show him this place.

You might even appreciate what he did. He told the boss to stick the afterlife up his... well, you know, where the sun don't shine."

The man smiled in delight and then let out a deep laugh.

"I must shake you by the hand." He grabbed my hand and pulled me over, giving me a clumsy hug. "So, you don't believe? You think that God is an oppressor and the afterlife is merely exploiting the people and keeping them down? The afterlife is not the disease but the symptom, like opium of the masses? Join me and we shall fight against him together. We should spread the message that spirits of the afterlife unite, as they have nothing to lose but their chains."

"You are one crazy agnostic", Cuthbert laughed.

"Steady on there, I wouldn't go that far, I don't want to fight", I held my hands up as if to physically hold his words back. "I was just upset that I died before my time, I didn't know if this was real or not. But now I know that it is I'm hoping it gets better."

"Hope. Hope!" he shouted. "You should never hope. Hope is futile, hope is what they want you to do while you are keeping quiet and getting on with it. People will put up with pain and suffering with nothing but hope to keep them going. You need to stand up and fight, only then will this end. All He wants is conforming puppets."

"Well, thanks for the advice but I think I'll handle it my own way", I smiled.

"Well, that's why I refuse to go back, if anything, He should come and apologise to me, I will wait till such time. Good luck with that my friend and remember there is strength in numbers; if you change your mind find me and we will stand together", said Karl as he stood up and walked away.

"Yeah, thanks again", I waved to him. I waited until he was out of earshot before I spoke again.

"Who was that nutter?" I asked Cuthbert.

"That was Karl Marx, I thought you recognised him."

"I thought it might have been by what he was saying but I wasn't sure. I take it he hasn't changed much since he was alive. How long has he been wandering around up here?"

"Over one hundred years now, since 1883."

"What, and he still hasn't accepted it?"

"No, some people just can't be taught. I just wanted to show you how clinging onto past memories and experiences doesn't allow you to move on to better things, it holds you back. Just admit they happened, learn from them and move on. Only then will you grow as a person and improve."

We started to walk down from the hill towards the tree we came from with Marx's words resonating in my ears. In truth I hoped I hadn't spoilt my chance with God and wouldn't get cast aside in this place to roam around in the nightfall.

"Oh, and by the way", Saint Cuthbert shouted over his shoulder to me. "Never ever make Karl Marx a pot of Earl Grey."

"Why's that?" I asked.

"He thinks all proper tea is theft." His head turns towards me, his toothy grin stretching wide over his face and he winked.

"I've got your slogan", I answered back.

"Oh aye, come on then let's hear it."

"How about 'The taste of paradise'?" I said.

"Aye, I kinda like that, cheers bonny lad." He patted me on the back as we walked off.

ACCORDING TO HARRY

The Archangel Michael and I appeared from a tree beside a busy street in London. I deduced our location from the black cab that drove by and turned into a side street. There were various shops; the usual newsagents, key-cutters and chemists. People walked by on their way to some destination or another, unaware of the two souls in front of them were on a mission of their own.

"So are you okay, McGroover?" Michael asked.

"Yeah it's been...". My mind raced to conjure up a word for my experiences since I'd passed over. Appearing outside an office complex, finding out I was dead, being offensive and upsetting to God, watching my own funeral, meeting various saints and visiting loved ones. One word seemed to fit but it didn't really do the whole experience any justice, still it was the only one I could think of.

"...Different, I suppose. I've learnt a lot, met some good people, but I do know I've done a few things that might not have been seen as helpful. I guess I will have to put up with what's coming to me."

He gripped my shoulders from behind with both hands and proceeded to give me a friendly shake.

"Don't agonise too much about it, Vince. Most things always work out for the best, don't you find that?"

"I'm surprised you're saying that to me, especially in my predicament. Where God is concerned I feel as though I'm a dead man walking, quite literally, so I'm not even going to dignify that with an answer. Where are we going now?" I asked, dismissing his cheeriness. It's easy to be cheery when your soul isn't on the line. Just because you have courage in your convictions and stand up for what you think is right and decent, some people always seem to attack that. I thought in the afterlife it would have been different.

"The Post Department", Michael said smiling and patting me upon the back.

"You get post?"

"Hmmm, well sort of, I suppose", Michael laughed. "Don't worry, you'll see."

We walked into what looked like a shop. There were pictures of horses jumping over hurdles posted on the front windows. Inside it was dimly lit, a few people either stood or sat around tables watching various television screens that were fixed high up on the walls. Most of the men were smoking cigarettes, creating a thick cloud that hung heavy in the air. For the first time since my death I was relieved that I couldn't smell anything back on this plane of existence. At least I couldn't die from second-hand smoke now.

"This is a betting office, surely this isn't an office of ours is it?"

"Yeah, you're right there Vince, this is most definitely not one of our offices", the Archangel Michael said as he glimpsed around, looking slightly out of place and as though he was feeling extremely uncomfortable. "But Harry does frequent this place in between jobs. The man likes to kick back when he can."

"Harry?"

"Yeah, you know Harry. I told you the other day. You remember God was speaking to him on the phone in his office. Harry or you might know him by his other name, Death."

"Oh yeah, actually, I have a bone to pick with him... No pun intended." I looked around the room and spotted two men sitting at a table. One was a middle-aged man, quite wiry, wearing a long black coat and a black porkpie hat almost hiding his black slicked back hair underneath. When the other man turned around I was shocked to see that he was slim and wearing a long black cloak; his white face had eyes lined with black to match his black lips, resembling a skull. I caught his eye and walked straight over to him.

"Hey Mr... Death, I think you owe me an apology. I know you didn't directly have anything to do with my death, but I am, as you can see, dead and as that is your department. I think the least you could do is say sorry or get me back somehow."

The man looked at me with sheer fear but did not speak, however, the other man sitting next to him spoke up without turning his head.

"I owe nobody a thing and by the way, squire, if you are looking for Death it's me who you should be speaking to. This is Eddie the Badger, and he's a

Goth and my runner. Now then geezer, what can I do you for?" The man spoke in a cockney accent that sounded more like an East End barrow boy than the raspy rattle of how I imagined Death would have spoken. He looked straight at me.

"Now, while we're doing introductions, my name is Harry and I suppose you already know my job title but just in case you don't it's Death, also known as Father Time and the Grim Reaper, which, just for the book, I hate. I mean, do I look grim?" he enquired, forcing a wide, cheesy grin to prove his point. "I mean, I'm positively chirpy, ain't I? Now that I've formally introduced myself, who might you be squire?"

"I'm Vincent."

"Ahh, you're Vincent, fair dues then. Guess I should expect the pain in the ear from ya, for what happened. What can I say, it wasn't my fault guv. Anyway look at you two, good to see you both." Harry got up and shook us both by the hand. He then turned to the other man who he was sitting with.

"'Ere Eddie mate, I'll see you later. 'Ere, stick 50 sovs on Dead-End for me for the 3.30 race. I'll meet you at the usual place."

The Goth took a large bundle of money from his coat and pulled out a £50 note. He left the table to fill in the betting slip. Harry turned towards us and saw the look of disbelief on my face.

"What? Hey, if I can't put some dosh on a nag with a name like that then who can, eh? ... Guys, come on", he grinned and spread his arms as if to inviting a hug from us. "Michael, squire, as if you haven't ever put a bet on." He then realised who he was speaking to, looked embarrassed and sniffed.

"Yeah, well... not like you haven't wanted to. But come on honestly, every geezer has his vice." He considered the blank expressions upon our faces. He quickly changed the subject: "Anyway, let me show you what I do. Walk this way, gents." Walking to the door, he picked up a clipboard from the table. Michael and I followed behind.

Outside the betting office Harry studied the clipboard. "Okay then, this is my clipboard of the jobs I have. Now, I only have two today, bit of a quiet one, but then again, if there were more, me being the boss and that, I can delegate to my staff can't I?"

He looked at me and winked: "Perks of the job isn't it, squire? Both of them not too far from here, which gives me a bit more extra time for some much-needed R&R or rather, back to the horses."

"So have you always been Death?" I asked as we walked.

"Oh yeah, I've always been about, I didn't always have staff though, but I found I was just far too busy, so the department grew just as the population grew. I'm sorry to hear you died the way you did, by the way. I personally didn't pull you but I guess I feel a little responsible that I or anyone from the department wasn't there. I'm sure you had all that explained, about us not having control of the animals blah, de blah, de blah, so there was no way of knowing. I'm sure we can sort something out though. 'Ere Michael mate, fancy a bet on the dogs this afternoon?"

"No way, I'm not betting with you again player. Last time we went to the dogs I remember what happened and that was not cool."

"What happened?" I asked Michael.

"It was one of his pickups."

"What, you kill dogs as well?"

"No, the dog wasn't his pickup, but his owner was", Said Michael, flashing Harry a suspicious glance.

"So what difference did that make?"

"The owner had a heart attack and fell on top of my dog, breaking its paw. I lost £20, so yeah, it made quite a bit of difference when you think about it."

"Hey, don't shoot the messenger Mickey, when it's your time to go, it's your time to go."

"You could have waited another minute until the dog was out of the way, that was whack jack."

"Time and tide wait for no man, geezer, you know what I'm saying. Besides, every cloud does have a silver lining, my dog won that race and I was 40 quid up", he laughed. "We're here."

I looked up and saw we were outside a greasy-spoon cafe, with a few motorbikes parked outside.

"What do we do now?"

"We wait; he should be out within the next …" Harry reached inside of his long coat and pulled out a silver pocket watch attached to a chain. "…Five minutes, give or take. You see Vincent, I always check the time on the clipboard with the time on my watch. Nice to be punctual ain't it?"

"Do you know exactly how he is going to die?" I tried to get a sneaky glimpse of what was written on the clipboard.

"Ah, ah, no, this ain't for your eyes Vince me old son, my eyes only I'm afraid. You see what's on here; I'll have to kill you. Oh no, you're already dead aren't ya! Sorry, just my little joke mate", he chuckled. "Take no umbrage guv. Oh yeah, I know, exactly, well it's all on the board and the board never lies." He tapped his clipboard with his free hand. Just then the door opened and a tall, wide, hairy biker, wearing leathers but no crash helmet stepped out of the cafe. "Yes, gentlemen, we have a flesh wad winner." Harry gestured both of his hands towards the biker as if he was a hostess showing off a prize on a TV game show.

"So, what do you do now?" I asked Harry, curious to see what happens when a life is taken.

"I just give their soul a tug, as simple as this." Death touched the Biker's shoulder. As he pulled his hand away a swirl of grey mist seemed to be drawn from the future deceased body. Unaware of his imminent death the man got on his bike.

"Cor mate, you really should have learnt to wear your crash helmet by now. That's the problem with people like that. They think they are too cool for rules, they always find out the hard way though", said Death shaking his head and watching the man climb upon his bike.

"Actually, speaking of which, when you came over did you see a light? Did you go towards it?" The biker started up his bike, which broke into life with a roar, shocking the people walking by. The biker smiled and laughed to himself, loving the fact that he could make people jump with fright.

"You forget, coming from England", I replied. " It's very rare we get to see anything that resembles sun. If I'd seen a bright light I'd have stripped down to my knick-knacks and tried to get a sun tan."

Michael wandered off to the stationery shop next to the café and peered through the window looking at the items on display. He shouted over to us: "I don't think I want to watch this guys, I never get used to watching anyone die, I'll... I'll just wait across here, I think".

Death looked over his shoulder to make sure Michael was not paying much attention to our conversation. I also looked back and saw him bend over and stroke a dog that standing with its two owners who were studying the café menu within the window.

"A word in your shell like, geezer", he said, slightly moving his body closer to mine, but still looking forward as if we were spies exchanging secrets in public.

"Tell you what, now he's out of earshot", he gestured his thumb over his shoulder, "Just to say sorry for you coming across and no one being there for ya, how about I'll do a favour? I'll kill someone for ya."

"What!" I 'whispered' loudly in disbelief just at the same time as the biker pulled away from the front of café straight into the path of a massive lorry. The vehicle screeched to a halt, but sadly it was too late.

Everyone within the vicinity who saw or heard the incident reacted. Some people screamed, some turned away in fear of what they might see, some hurried away, while others ran towards the accident in case the victim needed medical attention. I, however, stared at Death, shocked by what he had just offered.

"Ah fair point geezer, you were right, a helmet wouldn't have helped anyway", Harry said to the big, hairy biker who walked out of the crowd to stand next to us. "You can't argue with 20 tons of articulated lorry."

"What, so I'm dead?", the biker asked.

"Yeah, you're brown bread mate, 'fraid so. It's all over bar the shouting."

"So what do I do now?", the latest spirit asked.

"Well, you know when you are on an airplane and your ears pop, to make them un-pop you hold your nose and try to breath out as hard as you can", Death explained.

"Yeah?" the biker acknowledged.

"Well, you just do that, go on give it a whirl." The hairy biker did as Harry said and grabbed his nose with his right hand and tried to force the air out, this went on for a few seconds and nothing happened to the biker, who kept looking at us for encouragement. Until Death let out another laugh.

"As if it would be, why would you have to do that, are you always so gullible?"

The biker roared with anger and went to strangle Harry, who stepped back and held his arms out. "Now, now my son, just a little bit of levity to help the somewhat awkward situation. Don't go spare."

Michael turned around to see the commotion and stepped in between the two.

"Hey there, nice to meet you. Welcome to the afterlife. Can you see that door in front of us?", Michael pointed over to the wall of the café from which a glowing door had started to appear. "Now if you would like to step through it, one of your past nearest and dearest will be waiting for you to be your welcome host. I'd also like to take this opportunity to say thank you for dying with us and I hope your future in the afterlife is a safe and happy one."

The biker walked towards the pulsating door, opened it and vanished through the radiant glow.

The door faded back into the wall and vanished.

"There's always one with no sense of humour", Moving his coiled hand up and down in a stroking motion, Harry said: "Right then, are you lads ready? I've got another also-ran not far from here, so get ya boots on." He turned and walked off. Michael looked at me and shrugged, whilst I observed the scene in a daze, my mind thinking about the offer Death had just made me, wishing that it could have been something more in my favour.

We walked through the streets, Harry looking like he was on a mission, pulling out his pocket-watch again and checking it with his clipboard, while Michael ambled behind at a short distance, taking particular interest in the people and the shops we walked by.

I jogged to catch up to Harry.

"So this offer? You were serious? You'd... You know, kill someone... For me?"

"By what I've read in your file you always tried to help people and be kind to them, bar a few misdemeanours. A lot of people were unkind to you when you were alive and you didn't do them any harm. So just say the word and I'll do them for ya, then we can call it even for the mishap. But this is just between you and me, you understand?"

Harry moved his head in the direction of Michael and tapped the side of his nose with his index finger.

"Yeah, no problem, our little secret. But I can't do it; I couldn't be responsible for someone getting taken before their time. Two wrongs don't make a right."

"Well the offer is on the table geezer; just give me the nod if you want. 'Ere, the next person I have to tug is just around this corner."

We turned the street to find ourselves in a small park surrounded by black railings and tall three-storey houses. A few trees and small bushes were dotted throughout the green. Michael and I looked around trying to figure out where we could be going, not seeing a soul about.

However, Death seemed to make a beeline for a tree as if he could smell the life about to pass. We followed him, and as we moved around the large obstacle of a tree we saw an old homeless man who looked blue, his breath shallow, his body shaking. Harry tenderly touched his forehead and again a strange mist passed between the angel of sorrow and the dying man.

"Poor guy", Michael said. "Dying alone like this, no name, no one to miss him, no one to remember the life that once was. Some people etch themselves into our minds, some we try to forget, others just disappear without a trace."

"What happens to the homeless when they die, to their bodies I mean?" I asked to anyone that was listening.

"They get taken away and burnt, their ashes are scattered. It's sad really, a waste of a life." Sniffs Harry.

"Oh no, it wasn't a waste", the man uttered, as he sat up, stepped out of his body and stood by us. The four of us stood in a line looking down at his old body.

"Not a waste at all, I used to have a lovely family. Happy we were, had one beautiful daughter. I used to wake up every morning and be thankful I had them in my life."

"So where are they now?" I asked.

"Oh, they will be at home." He smiled as he remembered.

"I don't mean to pry, but how come you're not with them anymore?"

"Oh, it's a long story. I don't want to bore you with it." He looked at me with his piercing blue eyes and smiled.

"That's right, granddad, you know time's time. I've got stuff to do and souls to grab. Go on then, jog on, time to go through that doorway to your future", Death harassed the poor man.

I reprimanded him: "That's not nice, he does have feelings. I thought you would have had some compassion for the poor man. After all, aren't you a saint or something?"

"I'm an angel... technically. I was created for this job; to take souls out of bodies before they die. Look, I don't have a nice job, so I have to be hardened to it. Tell the truth, you look at a lot of people and it's truly not a shame they are passing over, they've really not done much with their lives. They'll push a few kids out, they'll be nasty to people and not care about anything other than themselves. It's hard to care sometimes."

"We don't know this man's story, but it looks like he's had it harder than some. Surely he should get some kindness at this time because it doesn't look like he's had much of it in life, not in recent years anyway. In fact, stay there." I ran off just before the homeless man stepped through a glowing door that had appeared in another tree behind us. "Hang on mate", I said, grabbing his arm. "Come on, tell us your story before you go."

"Really, you want to know?"

"Yeah, of course, come on."

Michael and Harry gathered around to listen to the story.

"Well, there's not much to tell really", the homeless man said, looking down at his feet. "As I said, I was married and happy but then the company I worked for most of my life closed down. I couldn't get work anywhere else because I didn't learn any relevant skills I could use anywhere else; that's what the job agents told me. I couldn't support my family any more. What do you do when you can't take care of the people you love the most? I found it hard to look them in the face. I felt as though I'd let them down. I'm not sure if it was the right thing to do, but it felt like it was at the time. I just simply disappeared from their lives. I left them, they were probably better off without a failure like me in their lives."

"Don't say that, you loved them, you cared for them. Losing your job was out of your control. Okay, maybe you could have handled it differently, but what's done is done.

"Did you ever think of what they would be going through not knowing where you were? Whether you were lying somewhere hurt? If you were alive? Probably not being able to get on with their lives because they hoped that one day you would walk back through that door. It's the not knowing that's the worst", I explained.

"I know, I know. I didn't know what else I could do; the longer the time, the harder it was to go back into their lives. I wish I could have done something to make it up to them."

"If you had the chance would you like to be able to do one last thing for your family?" I asked, curious about what his answer would be. I'd lost count of the number of times I'd heard people procrastinate in life. I know I had also been less than perfect in that department when I was younger. I thought back to when I promised my mother that I'd go to the hospital to see my Nan for two years and never got around to it before she died. I remember telling my cousins at their mother's funeral I'd come and stay with them, but with the best intentions I just didn't find the time. I remember telling Lisa Fletcher that I'd phone her after we spent the night together but never found the time to do it, well, that and the fact she snored. Or Vickie Thompson because she had a hairstyle like a witch. And Miriam Wilkinson, now I'm not saying the girl had a problem with upper lip hair, but every year people used to congratulate her for taking part in Movember.

"Yes I would, I'd give anything to make amends before I left for good this time, but I guess my time is over. I guess what's done is done." He looked down at his feet once again, his face reflecting memories full of regret.

A smile materialised across my face.

"Au contraire, mon frère, I think I have an idea which you might quite like", I patted him upon the side of the arm. I then turned around to Death, the same smile beamed across my face.

"Oh no, why do I get the feeling this is gonna be a little off-track and give me grief?"

I let out a genuine laugh and held my arms out looking like some cheesy TV host and smiling like a second hand car salesman.

"Nooo, it'll be fine, trust me. Anyway Harry, can I call you Harry?" Not waiting for a reply I danced around the question. "You know that you said you'd like to do me a favour? Well, I think I might be asking for it now, but on a good note, you don't have to kill anyone."

"Really?" he said in dismay.

Michael throwing him a shocked glance. "Really!"

"But killing is what I do best; in fact it's the only thing I do. I'm Death, it's why I was created, all I've known is Death."

"Well this time you get to act like a true angel of mercy, how would that feel?"

"Don't know really, never really tried it, I'll give it a go though, maybe... Should I?" He looked at Michael for support. Michael shrugged and nodded. "Count me in, I suppose." He sounded slightly worried.

"God, don't sound too enthusiastic, this is a good deed we're going to be doing", I smiled and winked at Harry. "First of all, we need your Goth friend Eddie. Will you be able to take us to where he is right now?"

Harry took out his pocket watch again. "Yeah, I think my last horse should have come in by now, so he should be in a graveyard not too far from 'ere. Come on then, I'll take you to him."

The four of us walked to the graveyard. On the journey I talked to the homeless man whose name, I found out, was Stanley Barker. He used to live in Stratford in the East End of London with his wife and their only daughter. He was a printer until the company went bankrupt and closed down. He's a nice man, I thought, the kind of man you would want as a neighbour, the type of man who would do anything for anyone; an honest, hardworking, family man who, through no fault of his own, is where he is today. If circumstances had been different for him work-wise, he'd still be alive and happy with his family.

We reached the graveyard to find Eddie, his back propped up against a tombstone, looking at an open newspaper and doing a Sudoku puzzle.

"Hey Harry, you got the double on the horses, you've won £500", he said as he looked up and spotted us walking towards him.

"A monkey, nice one. A good night at the dogs tonight I think then. But first, I hope you don't have any plans for the rest of the day me old son because we're in need of your assistance."

"Yeah, sure", Eddie said, setting down the newspaper, carefully putting the top back onto the pen and then into the pocket of his long black coat.

"Ah, don't put that away yet, we're gonna need it", I said, as he looked at me, then Harry, then back to me, with a blank expression.

"We need you to be a scribe and write down what this gentleman says", Death said.

"Yeah, okay", he nodded.

"And stick it into an envelope", I said.

"Yeah, okay", he nodded his head again.

"And deliver it." I say quickly expecting this one to become a problem.

"Ah, no way", he shook his head.

"Please", I begged. "None of us has the ability to deliver it, being intangible and all that, we need you."

"Address the letter, I'll buy the stamp and I'll

pop it into the closest post box for you", Eddie protested.

Death shook his head. "It'll take too long, his body will be cremated by the time it gets to the address. Go on Eddie, I told him I'd do him a favour-ish and, well, this is sort of it. I'll make it up to you, I promise."

"How?" he demanded.

"The next soul I take that no one knows but who has they have their own place, I'll let you squat there for as long as you can, it's well moody but it's the best I've got to offer geezer."

"Yeah, okay, I suppose." The Goth said reluctantly.

"Well, if everyone is agreed", I looked around, expecting someone to have a problem with the plan, but no one spoke. "Okay Stanley, the next part is up to you." He thought for a while and then spoke his piece as Eddie the Goth wrote it down.

After the letter was written, Michael and Harry put their hands on either side of Stanley's shoulders to comfort him.

"Are you all right?" Michael asked.

"Yes, I guess I'm fine, thank you. Can I ask, will I ever see them again?" Stanley asked.

"Yes you will, when it's their time and believe me they won't have lost any love for you when you see them either." Stanley smiled back, his face full of contentment by his final act and those kind words of hope from Michael.

Harry tapped him on the shoulder. "Come on chief, we have to get you back to the park and through the door, 'cos if I don't I'll be getting GBH of the ear hole from the boss. Anyway I think the smart money is on these lads to take care of everything."

"Actually Harry, one last thing before you go. His body will be getting cremated, could I ask for one last favour?" My words were sincere enough to hopefully find some way past the non-existent heart of Harry and sneak into where his kindness came from.

Death rolled his eyes: "Yeah I suppose so, while it seems I'm in a generous mood."

"The money you won on the horses, could we have it? It could go towards funeral costs, coffin, headstone, that kind of thing, you know?" I hoped he was feeling generous, that I hadn't overstepped the mark, especially as we'd only just met; asking a big favour for a man's soul he'd taken less than an hour ago.

Harry looked at Stanley, gave a deep sigh, then gave in.

"Yeah, okay, I suppose so, but that's us square now, right?" he said, pointing a finger at me.

"Totally, you're the best Harry. Thank you. Don't worry Stanley, we'll see that you get a real funeral with your family there and everything. You won't be forgotten, I promise."

We all said our goodbyes and went our separate ways, Death taking Stanley through the portal into a happier existence and leaving us to be the bearers of bad news.

Eddie, Michael and I were all standing outside the address in Stratford given to us by Stanley. Only

40 houses, 20 on each side, lined this small pedestrianised street, which had no gardens or gates, but front doors leading directly onto the quiet avenue.

"Okay, so what now?" asked Michael. "If Eddie delivers the letter, isn't that going to be a bit of a shock to the system, a stranger just turning up on their doorstep? They are going to ask some difficult questions, one of which will be about how he knew Stanley. I'm not too sure they'll like to hear: 'Hello, I'm a friend of Death and he's just taking your homeless father's soul. Anyway, be lucky'."

"It's okay, I've thought about that. Michael, you can do the whole laying on hands thing, can't you?"

"I haven't done for a few millennia, so I'm a little rusty, but yes, I can do it."

"Well, here's the plan. Eddie, if you go and put the letter on the doorstep, Michael you then go in and give them the magic hands to tie up the loose ends of the letter."

With everyone in agreement, each person played their role perfectly. Eddie put the letter into the envelope that we prepared along the way, placed it outside of the door, rang the bell and ran off down the street and around the corner just before the door opened.

A lady in her late 50s stepped out, looked up and down the street, noticed the envelope upon the stone step, picked it up, took out the letter and read it.

A younger girl in her mid-20s came to the door, and peeked over the other lady's shoulder. Seconds into reading it they both held each other, bracing each other as the shock of the letter hit them.

Seconds later they both started to cry. Finishing

the letter, the lady passed the younger girl the envelope and letter; she felt the money within the envelope and took it out to show her mother. Michael then stepped in to lay his hands upon them both. A physical shiver travelled down their spines as Michael passed on the information, and after a few moments walked away. Just as he got back to stand beside me the daughter said: "Mum, we need to go up west and get dad's body."

"I know", the lady said.

The letter read:

To Sarah and Chloe.

I am sorry I left you five years ago and I know those years must have been long and difficult for you both. I wish I could have saved you from that pain but sadly I couldn't.

When I lost my job I didn't feel like a man, father or husband anymore and it broke my heart so much that I couldn't be the provider. It felt as though you would be better off without me and that's why I did what I did. I know it was the wrong thing to do but as time went by it felt so much harder to walk back into your lives.

Things have been difficult for me since I left, but I hope that things became easier financially for you once I left. By the time you read this I will have left this world. Please know I am leaving it with regret for the hurt I have given you both. I hope your future brings you better times with much happiness.

Please know that both of you were always in my mind and not a single day went by that I didn't think about the love I shared

with you.
Please look after each other.

All my everlasting love,

Stanley.

ACCORDING TO SAINT KEYNE

I was lost in my own head, trying to make sense of the all the experiences I'd had recently. It still felt weird and unnatural not being alive, being in the afterlife. I know it's a cliché to say you never get used to death but that's always from the point of view of the people alive and left behind, maybe it's like that in death as well. Since I'd passed over everyone I'd met seemed to want to treat my death like retro trivia, almost like confectionery that has stopped production; you know, you enjoy it for years but then you don't buy it for a while and it mysteriously vanishes from the shelves. You don't notice until one day someone mentions it and you say: *'Yeah, I'd forgotten about those. I used to love those, it's a shame they're gone, oh well never mind'*. Then you carry on with your day. But to me it felt like losing a much-loved parent; it felt like a massive hole had opened and taken something special that could never be replaced; you never get over it, it just gets easier to deal with.

Michael and I journeyed through part of the afterlife, passing great lakes, some surrounded by grass, others by beaches. We saw animals from rabbits to camels; we passed tennis courts, golf courses and even a water park with giant slides and log flumes (where we saw the Queen Mother and Princess Diana). We walked into a thick wooded area full of animal life, insects climbing the vegetation and deer running through the trees, or rather around trees - rather than using the tree transport system.

"So, are you excited, Vince? You're about to see behind the scenes of one of the afterlife's secrets, what people have been searching for on Earth for hundreds of years, innit?"

"Yeah I guess, you are being slightly cryptic though, can't you tell me more about what I'll be seeing?"

His face became serious. "You really want to know? Fine." He hesitated looking deep into my eyes "The dark side of the force, the domain of evil it is, yet you must go."

"Really!"

"Na, I'm just messing with you Skywalker. Seriously bruv I don't want to spoil it for you. It'll be great, you'll admire in amazement, you'll shriek in surprise, you'll wow at the wonder, you'll gasp in...in...well, you'll just gasp. Honestly you'll love it, so hear me now", he said, finishing the last four words of the sentence like he was a reggae king while slapping his thumb, index and middle finger together in the air.

I stared at him for a moment before I spoke again, still confused about this angel - not just any angel - but one of the top angels, behaving like a cross between a surfer and a hoodie. "I'll take it from that I'll like it then?"

"Fo'shizzle you will, Vincey. Ah, here we are." We stood beside a huge tree that was as wide as a house and as high as the tallest tree I'd seen on Earth.

"Well, I'll leave you here Vince. I'll wait for you right beside this tree." He stuck out a fist: "Now hit me one, bro", so I softly punched his outstretched fist with mine. Then he sat down on the grass, using the tree as a back rest.

"Have fun, she's a character", he said and I gave a murmur of doubt thinking that sounded ominous. I looked closely at the tree and saw a door carved into the bark. "Go on, just walk in", encouraged Michael. I followed Michael's instructions and entered the tree by pushing the outline of a door.

Once inside, I closed the door behind me and looked around. It was a circular room with a large round table carved from the wood of a tree growing from the ground. The centre of the table grew all the way to the top of the ceiling and was a vibrant rich brown. Wooden chairs were placed around the table. Several cats walked around the room not paying any attention to my entrance, while two squirrels leapt onto the table and gazed at me. Unsure if I should approach them and introduce myself, I suddenly heard a woman's voice shouting loudly, coming from a room off to the left-hand side, which was separated by a curtain. I followed to investigate.

"God, have I just stepped into Narnia?", I muttered to myself as I walked up and pulled back the curtain, carefully stepping over a family of hedgehogs marching by my feet.

The offshoot of the room was of a similar size but this time an old lady sat in front of an old-fashioned telephone switchboard. She was small with grey curly hair and wore a green wool cardigan over a purple robe, which looked more like a baggy dress. Her outfit was topped off by a pair of purple furry slippers. She turned around as I walked into the room, smiled and waved at me, then held up her index finger and whispered: "I'll be there now, in a minute." She then turned her attention back to the exchange.

"Jeremy, Jeremy!", she shouted in a faint Welsh twang. "I 'ave to go now my lovely. I have a guest you see. I'll be back in half a moment." She took off her headphones, set them to one side, then got up out of her seat to welcome me.

"Ahh, now there, you must be Vance, I've been expecting you dear."

"Erm, no, it's Vincent actually."

"What?" she said, shaking her head and holding her right ear closer to me.

"You'll have to speak up. No need to whisper."

"No, it's Vincent", my voice slightly raised.

"Who are dear, you are?"

"Yes", I shouted, and nodded.

"Ooohh, dear me, I am sure they said Vance to me. I think they might have your records wrong. Maybe you haven't come up before your time my dear; maybe they just have your name wrong. You should look into that."

I nodded out of politeness.

"So have you been told what I do?" She shuffled across the room attempting to carry a chair over for me to sit down on, but instead scraped it along the floor making a noise like finger nails down a blackboard. My whole body reeled against the worst noise in the world - now understanding it to be the worst noise in the afterlife. The old lady didn't seem to flinch.

"I'm only small", she muttered placing the chair opposite hers at the side of the switchboard. She sat back down in her seat.

"Now where was I? Oh yes, cats, you're here to see my cat, he's been under the weather, you know."

"No!" I shook my head and shouted: "I'm Vincent, I've come to learn what you do."

"Oh yes, that's right deary. Well, I am Keyne, Saint Keyne. My father was King Brychan of Brycheiniog, have you ever been there?"

I shook my head.

"Ohh, have you ever heard of my father then?" Again I shook my head.

"Oh", she looked dismayed. "Have you ever heard of me?"

For the third time I shook my head.

"But in my innocence I didn't really take much notice of religions or saints when I was alive", I said, trying to make her feel better.

"Oh, not to worry deary, I suspect you young people have too much to do rather than want to know about us old people. You'll all be too busy surfing those cobwebs on that hairnet you young people love so much and watching those moving pictures on that television box or the TB, whatever they call it, or out at a concert dancing in the mosspit. Anyway, before I forget, would you like a mint?"

"Yeah, the living just love that old TB." I was half trying to assure her she was correct - not really wanting to offend her - and half being sarcastic.

"No thanks on the mint, not for me", I said as she

started to look through the many pockets of her cardigan, pulling what seemed like an endless supply of tissues and curlers out of them.

"No, okay, fair dues", she looked at me and smiled. "Now, did you come to see the roof?"

"No, I'm Vincent; I've come to see what you do!"

"Oh, yes, you know sometimes I would forget my own thingamajig. I'm so forgetful. Yes now, this in front of me is called a switchboard. I forget who invented this... was it you my deary?"

"No, it wasn't, I'm sorry I can't help you there", I smiled. "So, what does it do, do you operate the telephones for the whole afterlife?"

"Oh no dear, no, more important than that. You see, I handle all of the calls between the afterlife and Earth."

"All the calls? But people don't make calls to the afterlife." I looked quizzically at her.

"Oh yes, people do all the time. You get those people who try and contact the afterlife in a whole manner of ways, spiritualists, mediums, clairvoyants, psychics even those wheezy boards."

"It's a Ouija board."

"What is it dear, speak up?"

"It's Ouija", I shouted.

"Is it dear? Well, never mind dear, try not to pick it otherwise it'll not heal."

"No, I mean... Oh, never mind." I shook my head. "Carry on."

Another light blinked into life upon the switchboard, nestled among the others that had been flashing since I came in.

"Oh, now here we go, watch me and what I do." She put on her headphones with a microphone attached that stuck out beside her mouth. Then she plugged one of the jacks into the socket belonging to the flashing light and with the other hand flipped a switch so that the conversation came out of a loudspeaker so that I could listen in.

A middle-aged woman's voice came through the loudspeaker.

"Hello Kay, it's Jessica here. Are you all ready and set up?"

"Who's this?"

"Kay, it's me, Jessica", the voice shouted loud as if she was used to speaking to the hard-of-hearing Keyne.

"Oh, Jessica, now that's lovely. Have you come to speak to your daughter again?"

"Yes, well, try anyway." The voice said sounding full of frustration.

"Pardon?" Keyne enquired.

"Oh nothing, yes, I'm here to speak to my daughter."

"Let's see what we get this time my lovely." Keyne plugged a jack into one of the outlets belonging to another blinking light. She then clicked a switch and started to speak into her microphone.

"I've got Jessica here trying to get through to her daughter... oh, hold on. Jessica, what's your daughter's name again?"

"Matilda", the voice exclaimed.

"Yes, now we have Jessica, trying to get through to her daughter, Gilda."

A man's voice, presumably a medium from the land of the living, with an audience, sounded over the loudspeaker.

"I've got a lady trying to connect with me and

she's putting in my mind the name Gilda... does anyone know a Gilda?"

"No, Matilda", Jessica's voice bellowed through the speaker.

"No, sorry, Hilda", Keyne now instructed.

"No, not Gilda, I'm getting a Hilda, does Hilda mean anything to anyone? Someone in the back row there, yes Hilda... What was that? Hilda was your mother? Then I'm feeling this is the right connection. Okay, carry on my dear.

"What's your message to your daughter?"

"No, Keyne that's the wrong lady again, I came to speak to my daughter to give her the National Lottery numbers for next week."

"Okay lovely, leave it with me." She nodded, then turned her attention back to the awaiting medium and his adoring audience.

"She's mentioning pottery."

"Okay", the man's voice acknowledges. "Thank you spirit, now she's showing me pottery. What's that, your mother collected vases and jugs? This is great, it's undeniably the right connection then."

"NO, Kay, the National Lottery numbers, they are 24, 3, 6, 11, 36, 42."

Keyne reported back to the medium: "Number 24."

"Now the spirit is communicating to me a number, it's number 24... does that mean anything to you? What, your friend Edith lives at 24, that's great! Okay, let's see what else."

"Three", Keyne informed.

"Okay, I am now getting the number three. Does the number three mean anything to you my dear?" The Clairvoyant waited for a reply from the lady he was talking to. "No, well, try and think because I'm getting it strongly. What's that you've known Charlie for three years. Yes I feel it's him."

Repeating the order Keyne said: "Six, does six mean anything my love?".

A few moments pass as he awaits an answer: "Are you sure because I getting a strong number six? I'll tell you what, I'll leave that one with you and will you look into it my dear? Thank you".

Keyne followed up with "11".

"I'm getting 11 from the spirit world. Now it might not be a number, it might be like bingo, leg's 11. Is Charlie having problems with his legs?... No? How about his back? No? Well I'm feeling that he might have problems coming. Would you do me a favour darling and take Charlie to hospital when you get a chance as I think he might have the starts of rheumatism or gout? I get the feeling that Charlie doesn't want to make a fuss, he used to be very sporty when he was younger but now I feel he's getting on and still wishes he was younger. What's that love? Charlie's a cat. Erm, yes, well best get him checked."

"36, 42", Keyne continued.

"Now, the spirit is giving me a few things here. I'm getting two more numbers: 36 and 42. What? Next year you'll be 36. Okay, thank you and how about 42, are you understanding 42 my love?"

"No Keyne love, you've heard me all wrong again. Can we go to my daughter's husband, Terry", shouted the lady's voice from somewhere in the afterlife, trying to make her voice clear and loud in order for everything to be heard correctly.

Keyne nodded: "Okay my lovely, we'll move on. Was it Derek?"

"No love, Terry", the lady's voice explains loudly. "Eddie?"

"No, you're not hearing me correctly. Can you tell Terry about the lottery and then he can buy that new pool he's wanted for years." Jessica's poor voice now sounded as if she was shouting as loud as she possibly could.

"Okay love, will do, now are you sure that's the message?" An agreement came from Jessica, so Keyne agreed and then continued her conversation with the spirit whisperer.

"We're moving on now. Is the daughter's husband there?"

Yet again the man's voice echoed through the panel connected to the switchboard. "We are moving on to your husband, is he here with you in the audience? Yes, good, well there is a message coming through for him."

Keyne nodded ready to pass on the next piece of information. "Good, good my lovely. The message is that he's been loitering around a new school and that he's been wanted for years."

My eyes and mouth opened wide. A scream of "NO!" came from poor Jessica over the system. I grabbed the headphones from Keyne, almost garrotting her with the wires leading from them and plugged into the panel.

"No, that was the wrong message, can you just pass their mother and mother-in-law's love on to them and say that she misses them terribly. Thank you. Roger Wilco, over and out. 10-4, laters."

I signed off then yanked all the plugs out from the exchange, tapping switches up and down, not knowing what I was turning on and off, red and green lights flickering all over the panel.

"You can't say stuff like that", I said, my voice calm, trying not to scare the old dear whilst I untangled her from the wires and placed everything back onto the desk.

"Nonsense, I was just passing on the message, that's what I do my lovely. Now don't have a Cadillac arrest."

"A message is one thing but defamation of character is another."

"Ah, she's such a lovely woman that Jessica, would do anything for anyone."

"Well I'm not too sure she'll still be talking to you after that message you passed on", I said, not wanting to sound too harsh, after all I didn't want her to get into trouble with the big G.O.D.

I now understood why the living never, ever received important or life changing information from the afterlife. Nobody ever got messages from the afterlife telling them to get their heart checked out because next week could be too late, or be careful when driving your car on Tuesday as you might have an accident, or telling a man not to wear red trousers because it will just make him look like a dick.

It was always pointless things like change the light bulb in the hallway, you bought a new pair of shoes last month or do you know anyone with a D in their name. Keyne was that reason.

Suddenly, a voice came over the speakers; this voice was different to the last. It was a lady's voice; she sounded in her thirties and had a real caring tone. Although that wasn't what got my attention but rather the name she asked for.

"Your name is Paul Dabney and you're trying to

get in contact with Vincent Dabney is that right?"

I stared at Keyne in shock. Paul is my oldest brother. Like me he never believed in the afterlife or any kind of life after death and I was stunned that he was trying to make any kind of contact. I didn't move. I didn't know what to do. Do I make contact with my brother? Try to give him some comfort or let him go on believing that there is no life after death, that life is special and should be enjoyed to the maximum because you don't get another chance at it...unless you're Hitler!

"Sorry Paul, is there a message you want to pass on, I'm not getting anything from the spirit world." After a bit of a pause, the lady from the land of the living repeated what my brother must have just said. "You want to let your brother know that you miss him and he's left a big hole in your life, and that you wish he was with you now, especially at a time like this...now that your mother is in hospital."

And for the second time I was shocked. My mother, in hospital and I couldn't do anything to help. What was I supposed to do, ask how she was as if it was a phone conversation? Give him false hope and say it will be okay? Or say nothing and let him lose his faith but allow him to go on living his life?

Keyne plugged the headphones back into the single green light that was lit up on the board, she was just about to say something to the lady who was with my brother but I stopped her. I picked up the headphones and in a soft tone, just above a whisper, said down the microphone: "I love you brother", and switched off the green light.

Keyne's face suddenly changed from a light-hearted devil-may-care to being serious and stone-faced.

"I'm sorry to hear about your mother, my lovely."

My head dropped into my hands, I felt helpless. However it didn't stop Keyne.

"Now that we have some time together, I've heard that you have made a bit of a nuisance of yourself. Oh, you stick to your guns my lovely. My advice is never let anyone tell you what to do. It was your life they took from you and if you feel cheated then you have a right to be." I lifted my head in surprise at this eccentric old lady who was talking seriously and from the heart, totally different to what I'd witnessed moments before.

"Do what you feel is right in your heart and stand by that, have courage in your convictions and then and only then will feel that you never let your true self down. Your life was your life and your afterlife is your afterlife, no one can live it for you. You won't have anyone else to thank for the things you did or blame for the things you wanted to do but didn't; it's all up to you. You know life was too short to be afraid, so many people stay in their comfort zone, but we generally only get the best rewards and enriching experiences when we step out of those. Tell me, what are your goals up here, what do you want to achieve, what type of job would you like to do?"

"I... I... I guess I don't know, I haven't given it any thought I suppose."

"Isn't that why you are on this journey to find out what you want?"

"I don't know, I didn't really ask. I was just told I would be shown around and judged."

"Hmmm, isn't it the best time to start thinking about that before it's too late? I bet you can tell me that you have had a bit of a tough time so far? Hmmm, yes?"

I nodded.

"Well, adversity brings knowledge, and knowledge, wisdom. Think what talents you have, think about what you love doing, things people have told you that you are good at and something you would love to do."

"Well, when I was alive, people told me I should be a teacher, a nurse or a doctor. I was good with people. People always came to me for advice, plus I always put them at ease even during their most worrying times. I cared, I had compassion for others."

"And what did you do when you were alive?"

"I was a computer programmer", the words felt numb in my mouth, I felt as though I had to force them out of my mouth, as though I'd made a wrong decision within my chosen career. I had chosen a safe career instead of one that suited my skills.

"Well, I hope you still managed to find some enjoyment within it. I bet you were astonishing at what you did, I bet your achievements were huge and it made you feel important."

I looked for a sign of sarcasm in her face but there was none.

"No, I was okay at what I did, I wasn't bad, but I wasn't incredible. At interviews people would always ask me how I would rate myself as a programmer, but, I was never too sure who I compared to. I was better than someone that's just starting out but not as good as someone who's been doing it for 40 years, I used to tell them. They were never happy with that answer. How do you rate yourself? Why should people always compare themselves to others, life is not a competition. If someone came up to you and said as a person out of 10 how you would rate yourself? Nicer than Jack the Ripper but not as good as Mother Teresa?"

"But you showed pride in what you did, you were too proud to change that career maybe?"

"Not really, unemployment was my main motivation; wanting to give the things I never had when I was growing up to my future children was the other. But I never had any. I had modest dreams I suppose. I never wanted to be mega-rich. I guess all I ever wanted in all my life was for the people around me to be happy. Unfortunately, I always struggled to do that but I guess in the end I never got to achieve what I wanted, now I'm stuck here in this God-awful place. I would end it all if I could but as I'm already dead there's little point in that." My head looked down at my hands that were clutching each other.

"You shouldn't think of it as being stuck here, no man is a slave to anyone let alone a God, you are only a slave to yourself. Maybe it's not over yet", Keyne said. Her voice sounded full of sympathy. My head shot up to look at her but yet again she looked like she did when I first walked in, the subtle change I couldn't quite put my finger on.

"Oh, this place is just one big Trevor trove. Enough of that, now that I've shown you what I do that's the whole kitten caboodle. Would you like to 'ave a go my lovely?"

I began to shake my head.

"Oh, that's right, you wanted to come and look at my cat, he has been feeling under the weather today." Just then a light on the exchange lit up, this one was on its own, totally separated from the others. Keyne once again got on with her work. "Hello my lovely, okay, will do", was all she said before turning to me. "Well, your turn is now my deary. Remember what Shakespeare wrote in *Hamlet*? 'It's better to suffer the strings and arrows of mischievous fortune'."

I was just about to correct her but was thrown by her next sentence.

"That was God, He would like to see you now."

REVELATIONS

The sky was as clear and blue as far as the eye could see throughout the afterlife. It was the perfect day weather-wise but without the elements that cause any of the natural weather climates; sunny but with no sun, yet the temperature was just right. This wasn't Earth, it wasn't even Heaven, Hell, Asgard, Valhalla, Nirvana, Tian or in fact anything else, this was everything, this was purely and simply the Afterlife.

Michael and I walked through a small field. Behind us the office block that we had departed from just moments ago gradually faded into the background, as we wandered further through the pastures of the greenest grass I'd ever seen.

"What did you think of last night then?" Michael asked.

"Yeah, pretty amazing watching *Hamlet* with the real Shakespeare playing the part of Hamlet's father, how cool was that?"

"It's all good up here Vince. We appreciate the arts, beauty and general wellbeing. If you like theatre, wait until you see Charles Dickens in *A Christmas Carol* with real spirits. Or you could try rock-climbing, water skiing, river rafting, triathlons or yoga. If that doesn't get your juices flowing, our bridge evening is pretty popular. One piece of advice though, never have Judas as your partner."

"Why, does he cheat?"

"No."

"Does he get annoyed with the betting, you know, with the whole 30 pieces of silver thing?"

"No."

"Is he a bad loser?"

"No, He's just not very good. So it's your Judgment Day Vince, are you ready to start working here, to be part of us properly you jive turkey?" Michael now appeared to be going through a 1970s slang phase.

"As ready as I'll ever be I suppose. Even though I don't know where I'll be going or what I'll be doing, all I know is that I've angered God because of my thoughts and outlooks, so I'm pretty sure whatever I'll be doing, the verdict will be strict and unfeeling."

"Maybe you underestimate the mercy of God. Maybe you be blazing brother", Said Michael, briefly resting his hand on my shoulder.

"Be realistic, we were both there, He took a dislike to me. Anyway I think I've passed caring now. Who is He to pick and choose my life, my thoughts, what I can and can't do; I'm going to tell him to stick it. I feel like a man going to the gallows. I feel as though I'm a turkey a week before Christmas and on a drunken bet had the cooking instructions tattooed onto my chest, wearing a hat with 'Succulent' written across it, a coat made from bacon, shoes made from breadcrumbs and seasoning, and I've walked up to a butcher and called his mother a slut." I could feel myself shift into a semi-angry state.

"Perhaps you should just chill, listen to what He has to say and don't be too hasty. You saw the job He gave to Lucifer when she pushed Him and that was His best friend, so maybe it's not a good idea to go looking for a brawl Vince. Perhaps you should just be Snoopy cool, you know, silent but strong", Michael said. I had come to expect such a response from his permanent cheerful attitude.

"No, it's fine, He needs to be told a few truths I think", I nodded, trying to convince myself, whilst working up the courage to be argumentative while confronting my maker again.

"And here's your chance, but please be calm and it'll be all funkydory." Michael pointed towards two people; one sitting on a park bench, the other upon a sleek black bike like the one Steve McQueen rode in *The Great Escape* movie. Beside them was a large dog and a goat. The one sitting on the bench had long white hair and robes to match. I instantly recognised him as my antagonist, God. The person next to The Almighty was sitting upon the motorbike, wearing black robes, lilac-tinted sunglasses and several necklaces.

"Who's that with him?"

"Jesus Christ."

"All right, calm down arsey, I don't know all of the saints by sight. I mean the first time I saw you I wouldn't have known you from Adam, although after meeting Adam the other day I can clearly see the difference - nice to see him and Eve still together. Especially after she got him into all that trouble."

"No dude, I mean that is Jesus Christ."

"Really, he doesn't have the full beard? Just a

goatee, and how many crucifixes does one man need around his neck? He looks more like Johnny Depp then Jesus."

"Hey. He's a trendy cat that Jesus."

"Hold on", I stopped Michael in his path with an outstretched arm. "So you are telling me that is Jesus on a motorbike."

"Correct", Michael nodded.

"So that's literally Christ on a bike."

"Certainly is, where do you think that saying comes from? Anyway, man, this is where I say goodbye as your mentor." He took my hand and shook it. "It's been a real pleasure."

"Really, you have to leave me now? You're not staying to back me up?"

Michael shook his head, his hair bouncing healthily as if he was in some kind of hair commercial "It's all you now Vince, time to go out with your show out."

I gave a very half hearted nod to his enthusiasm. "Well, thanks for everything, I have really appreciated everything, you've been a great friend, I'm really going to miss you."

"Thanks, listen it's not like it's goodbye, we'll still hang out at night … depending on where you get placed."

I gave a weak smile, trying to put a brave face on the fact that I'd already resigned myself to the worst-case scenario.

"Yeah, sure. It'll depend on where I get placed."

We both patted each other on the back and he gave me a knowing wink.

"Don't think about it like you're a prisoner and your life has been taken away. Think about it as if this is a new start, but you can see old friends and family you thought you'd lost and make tons of new ones. You can learn from the best, you can meet your heroes and spend time with greatness. You've seen how fun it is here, make the most of it dude. Hey, just remember, it's all gravy baby. Just give them the Vince that I've seen all week and then you'll be sweet. Laters my man and remember to jive wise."

I watched Michael walk back towards the office block. I smiled, thinking of how good and kind he had been this week, looking after me and trying to take my mind off pining for my girlfriend. I wished there could be some way I could repay the favour. I then slowly turned and walked towards the bench where God and Jesus were chatting.

"Ah Vincent, how are you?" God asked in a cheerful manner, as I approached the bench.

"Yeah fine, for a condemned man", I said morosely.

God stood up from the chair without acknowledging my reply with an answer.

"Vincent, I want you to meet my son, Jesus."

I nodded my head towards him.

"Hi, nice to meet you."

"Hey", Jesus coolly nodded.

I looked at the very large dog with a large head, the coat smoothed close, flat and red and white in colour; its mouth slack around the sides and big sad eyes.

"And who is this fella? I've met a few of the other saints; I take it this is Saint Bernard?"

"No, this is Hank, he's just come by to say hello."

"How about the other fella, is he the holy goat?"

"Absolutely not", God shook his head, a wry smile appearing upon his face.

"It's another one of the things that was lost in

translation somewhere down the ages; you know what Chinese whispers are like, damn irritating. That's why I had to get Moses to write everything down; memory like a sieve. No this goat was supposed to be part of my whole message to Earth, however, my plans were ruined."

"Plans?"

"Well, when Jesus came back up to the afterlife, my next choice was to send the goat down to convince everyone. A talking goat that does miracles-- now who wouldn't believe there was a God then, eh? But then they started to call Lucifer the Devil and the Antichrist, I mean, she has her faults, but the Antichrist? You would have thought if there was an Antichrist, I, the all-powerful would have put an end to it by now. Then they chose the poor goat's face as a symbol of the devil. So if something resembling their image of pure evil turns up and starts talking … well, let's put it this way, I think goat kebab would have been on the menu", he said quietly while cupping his hands over the goat's ears.

"Anyway, what do you think of this place?" He spread his arms out as He talked.

My mind wandered, thinking how happy He seemed compared to the last time when He was annoyed and shouting at me. I then noticed that He was waiting for a reply for whatever He'd just asked. I tried to recall His last words in my mind. Was it about the goat? Was it about the dog? Oh... He said something about this place. "Erm yeah, it's, erm, long, it looks like it goes on forever."

"Oh no, it goes on longer than that. Look, I've got to sort out something for the goat, his name is Derek by the way, I'll be back in a minute", God said, excusing himself and the animals as they walked off together chatting (although I couldn't understand them, God was having a conversation with the animals just fine, unless he was as mad as Saint Paul).

I then realised that I'd been left alone with Jesus. I started to think, what do you say to Jesus? Just act normal I guess, what would you ask him if he was anyone else.

"I see Michael has done a good job of looking after you since your arrival." Jesus said.

"Yeah. He's a good guy…Erm…Saint, I mean."

Jesus nodded slowly: "You'll have to forgive his…funny ways. You know the whole surfer dude to American pimp speak. It's just he hardly gets to go down to the living world so he tries to pick up bits and pieces of slang up here and uses it to try to fit in with the people around him."

"Oh, yeah, I'd noticed", I said coyly. Then there was a silence before Jesus spoke again.

"He does a pretty piss poor job of it if you ask me", Jesus said, laughing as he fought to get the full sentence out, he looked at me and we both laughed.

"Well, I wasn't going to tell him."

"No, me neither, but he means well."

Once our laughter went quiet I paused for a while. "I have to admit, Jesus, you're not what I would have expected, I was expecting someone, less … well … less trendy. Not that I want to offend you, I'm just curious really. Just a matter of my own opinion, I mean the pictures on Earth of what we expect of you is someone, you know, more Jesus-ish. I'm not having a go at you, just interested."

Jesus was quiet for a while then moved his sunglasses down his nose to get a clearer view of me.

"Really, I thought I came across in the Bible as trendy, you know I started off geek chic, I'm très chic, I'm a bohemian, I'm like the Fonz in robes, I'm super-fly, the original pimp-father. Okay, let me ask you this. Who else do you know with an entourage of 12 guys, other than Puff Daddy or P. Diddy or whatever name he's using these days?"

"Hmmm, you do have a point." I was relieved that Jesus seemed really relaxed and not cantankerous like his father. He was soft spoken, polite, and there was an air of peace around him. I could understand why people followed him about.

"Have you had a good time up here, so far?"

"Yeah it's been okay. I miss my life though", I said with a sigh as I sat down on the bench. "It's all a bit of a whirlwind really. Even though it was a lot longer it only feels like four days ago since I died and I've been pushed from pillar to post, plus I don't think your father likes me. I've seen some pretty amazing things though: the snowfields, Mary, sorry, your mother, singing karaoke, even Shakespeare in an actual Shakespeare play. Yesterday I spent ages sitting in one of the oriental gardens beside B block, it was beautiful."

"Oh, you've seen nothing yet , there is so much more to discover, this place is 100 percent amazing, which is why I was trying to tell everyone on Earth about how good it is. I guess I was the original holiday rep."

My head slumped down towards my chest.

"Not that this is a holiday."

"No, of course not, but we've got masses of amazing things up here, some of which you've seen already. We've got a massive beach, a great library, an

Olympus-sized swimming pool."

"You mean Olympic."

"No, I mean Olympus, it's huge. Of course things change all the time. Where you are standing now used to be an amusement park."

"Really?"

"Yeah, it was originally called God World, but we thought it was a bit pretentious, so we went with Testament World. There were some excellent rides. The Noah's Ark attraction was amazing fun, if you love water rides."

"So what happened to it?"

I always was interested in history and this was history - you couldn't just pick up a book and learn about it, which made it like finding a treasure chest of facts.

"Well, we kept wondering why most places looked empty, we couldn't work out why the attendance figures were up but most of the park looked empty. We eventually sussed out that everyone was going to Sodom and Gomorrah Land. You think he's upset at you, you should have seen him then. He just flipped out, went mental. So He closed the park down and built this land, or rather, extended it."

"Yeah, it looks nice and there are good things up here too but I guess I miss Earth, I miss my friends, I really miss my fiancée, I even miss having a job." I went quiet for a while, thinking of all the things I missed.

"So how about you, do you miss being down on Earth?" I asked Jesus.

Jesus' head nodded to motion a yes then he turned it into a shake of a no.

"While it was pretty funky, I don't think so, not

really, and I didn't really see it as a long-term thing. Yes, I was surprised that it was so short but these things can't be helped. I won my bet anyway."

"Bet?", I was taken aback.

"Yeah, I had a bet with Moses that I could save more people than him. We went about it totally differently. He was a bit too heavy handed, got into fights, even killed one guy. He was tooled up though, he had a staff that turned into a snake, could turn water into blood and parted the Red Sea.

Whereas I went down all sweetness and light, you know, took the peaceful stance, healing people, changed water into wine and raised people from the dead. Okay, he saved his people but look at how many people I've saved and still saving and I haven't even been there for most of it; but I'm still bringing them in. See, it's all about the long game. Which just goes to show, you can catch more bees with honey than you can with vinegar."

"What, so it was all just a game?"

Jesus shook his head and moved his weight on his bike.

"Oh no, not at all. We were trying to get the message across, man's salvation, love each other and everything else. I gave them the flesh of my flesh and heart of my heart. We just had a bit of a side bet to make things interesting. At the end of the day I got the numbers so I won. He was a bit of a div though. Typical guy, he wandered around in the desert for 40 years, 40 years! Just because he wouldn't ask for directions; too proud you see, all ego, he kept going around in circle."

"So what did you win?" I asked, closed my eyes and shook my head in total disbelief of the historic events I'd just being privy to.

Jesus took the lilac-tinted sunglasses off his face, and motioned his eyes down to his bike.

"It's pretty cool, you have to admit."

"Well I hope it was worth it", I said, my voice not disguising the annoyance.

"Hey, don't be like that man, what we had to do we did with our heart, and it was our job, our life, our whole purpose. The bike wasn't part of the bargain, we just said the winner would get a prize. For me it was this bike. I do wish more people had listened though. Just look at how many have been killed in the name of my father. I mean look at me, I went down there, never hurt a fly, in fact I did good all my life and what happens, I get punished and killed. But people always seem to persecute and murder the people trying to spread the word of peace."

"Yeah, I know, you for a start, Gandhi, Abraham Lincoln, Martin Luther King, John Lennon", I agreed.

"And that is just some of the famous people; there have been thousands of unknown people that have being killed for the peace they believe in. I used to wonder if it was worth it, you know, me dying to show people the way."

"And?"

"I came to the conclusion of course it was. Even if I had just got through to one person, who would stand up for what he believes in and acts out of love for his fellow man through care and consideration, hoping that would inspire others, then it was all worth it. There is so much hatred in the world though. It makes us so sad up here. Look at every war. We watched them all happen."

"Couldn't you stop them?"

Jesus dropped his head down towards the ground and sighed.

"We did try during the First World War, we sent some angels to Mons in France to help the British but then we held a committee meeting and decided that we can't just turn up and take sides. Can you imagine how much worse that would make things? Instead, we just had to sit and hope for the best. He cried you know."

"Who did?"

"My father, our father, God. He cried. So many lives taken so needlessly." He shook his head thinking, recollecting his memories of everyone in the afterlife watching down on the atrocity below.

"Why can't people just think about the damage they are doing both to themselves and others?"

I shrugged, "I think they do consider the damage, they just don't care as long as they get what they want."

"He gave humans a beautiful world to live in. He's tried so hard to make things right, but I guess at the end of the day man's inhumanity to man is stronger than even his power."

God returned, walking towards us, shook his head and laughed at the two of us sitting on the bench.

"Well, aren't you two a cheery couple."

"I was just telling him about World War II", Jesus pointed towards me while picking up and undoing a black and silver record bag that would look at home on a dispatch rider. He took out a package wrapped up in silver paper and handed it to his father.

"Yes, it was sad but it's all over and forgotten now, so no good dwelling on the past now is there. Vincent, walk with me a little", He said as he placed the package under his arm and the other over my shoulder.

"Yeah, I've got some stuff to take care of. If you'll both excuse me, I'll see you later, Dad." He shook my hand with his right hand and covered the back of my hand with his left. "I've got to get my hustle on. Hey, take care and keep the faith. Oh, and by the way, Dad, the actions you're about to take, I think you're correct."

"Yeah … Bye … Jesus. What did he mean by that?" I turned to ask God. Jesus started up his bike and sped off, doing a wheelie as he disappeared into the trees beyond. We both started to walk for some distance through the grass, which spread out and surrounded a pond and then we stopped. Birds from the surrounding trees were gently singing their songs. If I could give this place a name it would be Contentment. I kept on looking at him, awaiting an answer.

"Patience, Vincent, in good time", God said, patting me on the back and finally answering my question.

"I still can't believe that was Jesus!" I exclaimed.

God laughed: "I thought after your past few days of meeting the saints and the angels you would have gotten used to it?"

"I thought I had", I said. "But I've just spoken to Jesus!"

My finger pointed in Jesus' direction, still hearing the engine of his bike in the distance as he sped through the forest.

"And now you're talking to God the creator. I always come here to think. I was so proud of my invention of nature, so relaxing don't you think?"

God asked, his voice full of compassion.

I was slightly taken aback, I had to admit, I wasn't expecting God to be this friendly, I thought I was going to get judged and punished immediately. Perhaps He's just trying to catch me out, perhaps it's the final part of the test, best keep on my guard, I thought to myself. "Yeah, it's nice and tranquil, it's quite a size. I would hate to be the gardener though!"

"Don't need one, the animals look after that for us."

"The animals?" I repeated.

"Yes, the goats, sheep and others all do their bit, that's their job up here, if you like. Speaking of animals, I remember Noah when he told the animals to go out and multiply. The snakes did have a cheek; they turned around and said that they couldn't multiply. When he asked them why they said because they're adders", God said looking at me and waiting for a reaction.

"What really?" I said, genuinely interested.

"No, that was a joke", He laughed cheerfully. "Sorry Vincent, I don't mean to laugh at you, I didn't think you would be that gullible."

I looked at him feeling embarrassed. "I'm not sure what to believe sometimes with some of the things I've seen and heard since being here."

"You know Vincent, you are right, you've come a long way since you came up here and you've had to learn a lot in such a short space of time, which brings me to my next point. You now admit that I exist?"

"Yes, I suppose I do now. I'm sorry about what I said back in your office."

"That's fine, to err is human, to forgive is divine, you know. It's the end of your probation period, but before we get down to business, I'd like to ask if you have anything to say for yourself."

I thought for a moment then shrugged.

"Well, I didn't think it would be like this, it's just like living. I thought I would have, I don't know, I guess I thought I would be more in control, you know with the job? Plus I thought there would be some final…finality, you know? Some purpose to it all."

"Hmmm, I see, but let me ask you this if you will. You aren't totally in control of your life on Earth, a lot of it depends upon the people around you, your surroundings and luck, so why should the afterlife be any different?"

"I don't know, but then again I don't know what life was all about."

God shook his head.

"People are always in search of what life is all about instead of just living it. Animals don't sit around worrying about what may or may not be, apart from tortoises, they worry their little heads off, no wonder they all look old before their time."

"I guess people have just forgotten the meaning of the message you wanted them to live by."

God let out a little snort of laughter.

"I don't know how, it's all around them, it's inside of them, in fact it is them. I mean look at food, I give them lovely fruit and vegetables, even animals and fish to eat. What happens? They find rubbish to eat like mushrooms … I mean, mushrooms. It's a fungus; same as truffles, and people pay a fortune for them, you don't eat fungus, oh, and don't get me started on people who drink their own urine." He shook his head in annoyance.

"I think people are always after something new, something exciting to try. If they didn't, then nothing would get invented, nothing would have been made. We would all make do with what we had already, we'd stagnate as a race and probably still be cavemen. Perhaps if people knew all of this was waiting for them then they would respect life a lot more", I pointed to the space around us. "You know, let them see what the afterlife has in store, a sort of try before you die."

"No, that's totally the wrong way around, it's not about what waits for them in the afterlife, it should be about what life is about. I agree that I look around the streets and people are always complaining that they are lost within themselves but they never listen to themselves. What did you think déjà vu was, just a bit of fun?"

"You mean it actually meant something?" I asked.

"Of course it did, it was a way of telling people that they are on the correct personal track of their lives, that they are going the way that they should be."

"Hold on, so are you saying our lives are all planned out?"

"Certainly not, that's why you all have free will. If I wanted puppets, I would have made puppets but I didn't, I created people with hearts and minds and freedom of choice. Now what I am saying is there are things in life that we are supposed to do, not everything but some things. It's more of a guide for yourselves rather than an order from me. Besides, you choose it yourselves."

"I still don't get it, I'm sorry if I come across as a bit slow", I said, not grasping the concept that God was explaining, then again it was the explanation of life, which I wasn't sure should be an easy concept to grasp.

"Well, when a soul is born into the world it makes choices", He explained.

I scratched my head while trying to get my mind around this fact.

"What, like from an Ikea catalogue?"

"If you want to use that analogy then, yes, like from an Ikea catalogue." He reiterated: "And the soul gets to choose the life it wants in order to be happy or the life it wishes to try. It then makes a list. The soul and I then have a consultation with a slideshow so that I can show and tell what it needs to do in order to obtain that life. But when the soul is born it forgets all about the discussion, yet deep inside that information is stored. What it forgets with its mind it remembers with its spirit".

"Oh, I get it, so when you get a feeling of déjà vu it's just that memory rushing back to the surface and that's how you get the feeling of it happening before", I nodded hesitantly, hoping that I'd got the right end of the stick.

"Precisely my boy, and that's why it only lasts a second or two, just like a slide within a slideshow. But a lot of people just forget about it all together, they never really tune into themselves, they get too selfish. They never really respect themselves, their bodies, other people, or the Earth for that matter. You know life should just be about enjoying it and allow others to enjoy it with you. Be free, happy, improve yourself and allow others to improve themselves around you. Look after yourself, each other and the world around you, it is as simple as that, nothing difficult. Look at you, you made a wrong choice in life."

I contemplated this for a few moments; the first thing that sprang to mind were my last precious moments on Earth.

"What, you mean going on holiday and dying? That was hardly in my control."

"No, I'm not talking about that, I mean you had a few chances in life to make something of yourself but you took the wrong path."

"Well, I didn't have a good start in life, I did go to the worst school in England; in fact it's shut down now because it was so bad. One of the television channels did a documentary about it once and the reason it was so dire. We were the only school in the district with an obituary column in the school magazine and in the school car park we had our own space for an ambulance because it was there so much. We had a truancy rate of 30 percent."

"Thirty percent is not so bad."

"That was only the teachers, the kids were much worse."

God laughed.

"I know that school and it wasn't that bad and you were surrounded by some great pupils and teachers that cared. Regardless of where you came from you still had choices in front of you, which you never did make the most of."

I scratched my head thinking of various times in my life when I had big choices to make and it all went wrong for me.

"Ahh yes, I did try to write a book about what it would have been like if great people like Shakespeare or Martin Luther King were born into today's generation, it was called '*iPad a dream*'.

I tried my hand at a few E-books online, books

like *'How to give a rabbit hernia'*, *'How to chat up a nun'*, *'How to put wheels on a dog'*, *'How to sleep with someone you're not attracted to'*, *'How to wear a coat'*, *'How to look like a king'*, *'How to spot a queen'*, *'How to get into Scotland'*, *'How to get out of Wales'*, *'How to live in Scunthorpe'* and *'How to bully the catatonic'*, but none of them made a penny.

Then I tried to become a writer for TV, it was a comedy show about a man who was accident-prone set in the trenches of the First World War."

"And what happened there?".

"Well...the television producers said they didn't like the title, it was called *'Somme mothers do 'ave 'em'*, they said it was all in bad taste. I did think about setting up a shop, which was going to be like those places where you stick your feet in a tub and fish bite the hard skin off your feet only my idea was with moles instead of fish and haemorrhoids instead of hard feet skin, it was going to be called Mole-asses. I then tried to set up my own website company but that went all wrong as well."

God looked at me, smirking as if He knew what I was about to say already. "Oh, and what happened there then?"

"Well, the first job I had was from a company called Automated National Knowledge. It was a company that built knowledge management systems for government departments, it was based in Africa in a place called Eritrea, I'd never heard of the place before."

"Carry on", He requested.

"Well, it was all going really well, the website was completed, I said I'd take care of the whole domain side of it and things and that's where it went, well, a bit wrong. You see, you know the domain for company is .com, for the UK it's .uk, for France it's .fr and so on? Well the domain for Eritrea is .er."

"Yes."

"Well, it made their website address www.ank.er. I never noticed, I guess I didn't think. They didn't notice for a while either to be fair. Even though their poster campaign should have highlighted the problem, their posters and leaflets read 'Let our business be your business because you deserve it www.ank.er'. Well, that's when it got into the newspapers, I don't think it would have been so bad but the managing director had a stutter so I think he thought I was teasing him. So that was the end of my web company, no one would touch me with a pole after that. In between all of those disasters I worked for companies that wanted me to do the work but not improve my skills and they held me back."

"You didn't make the correct decisions, it was your choice of career from the start, you were about to graduate from university and you were going to become a teacher but you didn't, even though you had people around you - who knew you better than anyone - telling you that you would make a great teacher, nurse, social worker or something with people. You were caring, considerate and you looked after people, but you didn't listen to those friends."

I broke eye-contact and started to look at the space around us trying not to look as embarrassed as I felt.

"Yeah, I know, I didn't get into teaching because the money is bad, I was getting double what teachers make in the outside world."

"But it never felt right did it? All the places you

worked you never settled in."

"No, you are right, it didn't feel right, but I had to keep going because of my reasons for going to university at the beginning."

"Which reasons were they?"

"That I wanted a family one day and wanted to give them the things that I never had when I was a kid: a nice house, nice clothes, a good school and to go straight to university and study something they want to and not because they have to."

"So you sacrificed your happiness, your future, your natural choice in life for their happiness?"

"Yes, for the greater good, at least in my eyes. Anyway, that is all redundant now; I'm dead and never had that family I wanted." I heaved a sigh and looked down at the grass, I felt that my whole life was all in vain, a waste of hard work, very hard work.

"Maybe life is just about enjoying it the best we can, no matter what obstacles get in the way of our dreams. These obstacles are to be lived through and are not simply problems to be solved."

Silence fell between the two of us for a while.

"I was going to be a writer for the world, you know", God said, breaking the silence. "I mean the Ten Commandments, there was going to be a lot more than ten, even the name 'The Ten Commandments' was different, it was originally going to be called 'Everything you ever wanted to know about life but were afraid to ask'."

"So what happened?"

"Well it was the editor, Moses, he chopped most of it out, changed the title, there were some really important messages left out like Commandment number 15: "Thy shalt not destroy the Earth's layers", meaning the ozone layer, but I guess he cut out what he didn't understand, you know what editors are like, they always think they know best."

"Yeah and humans are destroying the Earth", I agreed sadly.

God let out the loudest laugh that I'd ever heard not only heard coming from him but out of anyone in my life.

"Destroying the Earth, oh no, they'll never do that, even with the diminishing ozone, melting icebergs and countless other ways they are bringing it harm."

"Yeah but..."

"Nonsense, I built in contingency, don't underestimate my level of planning and intelligence for everything I have created. Do you know how clever the human body is? The left lung is smaller than the right lung to make room for the heart; the life span of a taste bud is ten days but the cells are constantly being renewed, roughly one every hour; the liver has over 500 functions.

Look at how amazing a piece of cow dung is, around it the grass feeds and grows high, on top of the dung fungus grows, the hat-thrower fungus. When this fungus is ready the hats pop off over the long grass on to fresh grass, which the cows then eat and it starts all over again, continuously feeding and giving nutrition. Cows and dung helps the increase of insects to over one million per cow, which feed from the dung, and birds come from all over the world to then feed off these insects. You see, it's all one big chain, one animal helping another.

Now, listening to those few facts did you think it was all by mistake, by chance? The planet is fine. It's the people of Earth that are in danger. Look, the planet has been around for about four and a half billion years, humans have been around for a relatively shorter time than that. The planet has been through a lot worse than humans and their carelessness; it's been through earthquakes, magnetic storms, plate tectonics, sun spots, cosmic rays, continental drifts, it's had comets, asteroids and meteors hitting it, volcanoes, floods, fires and ice ages. Do you think some plastic bags, milk bottle cartons, polystyrene and deodorant is going to hurt the planet?

I went quiet again while pondering. "...Yeah but...".

"The Earth isn't going anywhere. It's humans that will end up like the Dodo, the Bali Tiger or the Thylacine, just another failed organism, if they don't clean up their act. The planet will heal and cleanse itself and adapt to what's happened to it. I do know what I am doing and for those who don't think I do I will say only this, 'O ye of little faith'."

We continued to walk. "Humans have forgotten what life should really be about. They should learn from the animals and nature I created around them, none of them take more than what they need from the resources. The animal kingdom is led by democracy and co-operation yet humans have turned it into a world full of competition and greed, from sports to business. Humans used to fear their gods and some used it to control others, when they couldn't do that anymore they made their own power to control others and that was the economy, now it controls the world but it's a man-made demon."

"So why don't you do something about it instead

of watching everyone suffer? I mean you complain that people don't believe in you but you've not done anything through the ages to help that cause."

God smiled.

"I'm doing what any good manager does; I'm keeping out of it until I am truly needed. There are a lot of good people on Earth and I intend to let them go with it, you see, it's all about timing and trust. Just like in any relationship between humans. Just like a relationship between a person and a horse. Have you ever ridden a horse, Vincent?"

"No I can't say I have."

"Well, I learned in the early days if you pull too tight the horse will bolt. I made the world with love. The very same as a couple making a baby with love. When it's born you can't control it, you have to give it room to grow and learn for themselves, good and bad... if you follow my meaning?"

I nodded: "So how about Moses making all those changes to the Bible, also I've heard since coming here that some of the Bible is wrong but some is right, what were we supposed to believe?"

"Well... for a start, maybe you are asking the wrong question."

"Wrong question?"

God pondered for a moment: "Let me ask you this, do you think that the Bible was trying to tell people to love each other and themselves."

"I guess at the crux of it, I suppose."

"Well, that's all it ever was supposed to do. Yes some of it got lost in translation, but then again people just cherry pick what they want from it anyway, but all I wanted was for everyone to live in peace and harmony."

"How about people that commit suicide, why aren't they allowed in Heaven?"

"Oh, they are. Of course they are. Why wouldn't they be? I know that life is a gift but people that commit suicide usually have had such a hard time caused by others, a run of bad luck or in very poor health and sadly can't face the pain of life anymore. Doesn't it make sense that that I wouldn't welcome them with love and open arms to a better place where they can be happy and healthy? I mean, come on, just because it's a gift doesn't mean that everyone has to like it. A wig for a cat is a gift, doesn't mean everyone will like it."

"You've been talking to Cuthbert haven't you?" I ask, he nodded with an uncomfortable look upon his face. The conversation then went silent for a while.

We turned around and started to walk back towards the group of buildings.

I thought now was the time to speak up regardless of the consequences and confront him. "So how about me? Am I just going to be cast aside by you just as the planet will be cast aside by the people? I have to admit and at the risk of sounding like a stuck record, I really haven't liked the blasé way my death has been treated. All I wanted was an apology from someone or someone to care, but instead I guess you've judged me and now I'll get punished by you."

"Ah yes, punished. Let's look at the facts since you've been here shall we?"

"Hmmm or we could just bypass ... them", I say wrinkling up my face while shrugging my shoulders as if there was nothing important to talk about.

God didn't listen. "First of all shall we start with

Lucifer and upsetting her by going on and on about how evil she was supposed to be."

Chipping in with my defence: "well, to be honest I can't take all the credit for that. I think you partly…"

"Then the visit to Paul and getting involved in something that you shouldn't have.

Cuthbert and passing thoughts to your girlfriend, misusing the power Paul had given you."

"…Yeah but…" I squirm.

Ignoring me God carries on. "Oh and then there was Harry and again getting caught up in something you had no right to and implicating poor Harry and his friend as well.

The rudeness you showed poor old Keyne not mentioning the rudeness you showed me when we met."

"But what you don't understand is…" my brain had nothing in the form of an excuse for any of it other than trying to do good.

"Vincent I've always known what you were going to do."

"Yeah, treat me like a second-class citizen and be punished for nothing." I was now really on the defensive waiting for the next comment from God so I could get a few more verbal digs in.

"Vincent you should remember Commandment number five. Honour thy father and mother; am I not the Father of all that is in Heaven and on Earth?"

"I guess you're right… I'm sorry, I was still trying to come to terms with being here, I didn't mean to be rude and no one really seemed to be helping."

"Of course I am, I'm God, I'm always right, but yes there was no excuse for my temper either. I was strict in the beginning when the world was new and I guess I find it difficult sometimes to show the fundamental characteristic that is within all of us. One of the most important qualities within the human race, in fact it's so important to humans it's named after the word... humanity", God smiled.

"Yes well, I think we've both found a little of that lately", I said, smiling back at God.

"You are not the first person to lose his temper at me, oh no. The worst one has to be the philosopher Friedrich Nietzsche. Well, he thought he was the Antichrist for a while, he even wrote a poem called Madman and in one of the verses he wrote, '*I seek God*'.

When he died and saw me for real, in the afterlife, it was a bit of a shock for him. He always said that people had killed God but you can't kill something, which doesn't die, in truth you can forget about it or even lose it... it doesn't mean it's not there.

One thing that he wrote did bother me though that the '*Death of religion is freedom, that the church gives people morals*'; However, that is everything I didn't want, following something out of fear, I wanted them to follow because it was in their heart and soul."

"But isn't that why you put me through the last few days to teach me a lesson, and a harsh one, if that, so then you could stick me in Hell out of the way of everyone."

"Do you think you deserve to go to Hell?"

"I don't know. I'm not a murderer but I didn't believe in you when I was alive and I've gone against the rules since I've been here."

"'*No man can enter heaven until he is first convinced he deserves hell.*' John W. Everett said that."

I looked at him blankly and just shrugged my

shoulders.

"Yes Vincent, I did test you, but not in the way you think. I was shocked at your outburst and wasn't too sure. I knew the correct role was waiting for you but because you came up so early I wasn't sure if within yourself you were ready for the job, not yet.

I had to make sure that you had it in your heart to do the correct thing in death as well as you did in life, especially when it felt you had nothing more to lose. But I know that I chose correctly, after all, don't you think that I, your creator, can look deep into your soul and know and understand you totally? You think I'd punish you in the afterlife because you broke a heart or two, or stole a pound from a sideboard when you were eight years old and knew no better. People think I get so upset at such small things", He said looking into my eyes.

I suddenly felt humbled.

"You see, I was trying to tell you all the time what I thought would be a good job for you but you wouldn't let me finish what I was going to tell you and then you kept throwing insults, so I needed to make sure you were in the right frame of mind and correct stage of your life for this important role. I tested you throughout your time the last few days."

"Yes and by what you said before it sounds like I failed all the tests by upsetting everyone and getting involved where I shouldn't have."

"Well, let's look at the true evidence, shall we. Let's start with Lucifer. Robert Spring offered you another body and riches, you declined, so there you resisted not only gluttony and greed, but you showed honesty."

"So he was part of a test? I had a sneaking

suspicion it was."

"Actually, no; But he did serve a purpose; he will be dealt with for his malevolence... once we catch up with him. However, that is not your problem. Anyway, I digress. Next there was Saint Paul and yes, I know what happened on the escalator and you did show diligence but you also did not let sloth get in your way.

Then Saint Cuthbert, there you didn't give into lust but you did show humility.

Death offered you something shocking in the name of envy and instead you gave a stranger generosity, and Keyne asked you about pride but you gave her patience."

"Isn't there something missing?"

"Well, maybe with me it could have been so easy to show wrath but what I saw was courage, it's not easy to stand up to the most powerful being in existence." He winked.

"Well ... I... I", I stuttered, totally lost for words.

"Look Vincent, you've been taught by the best over the last few days, but I've always needed someone in a position that you've just seen the others in these last few days. They've been the guide to the new, inexperienced souls.

Everyone you have met to guide you will be the first ones to agree that they don't have the compassion to show people around, to initiate them, especially the ones that come up before their time. Yes, the angels are great but they have never lived and therefore don't understand the loss, the sheer desperation mortals feel.

You, Vincent, you do. You have a kind heart, you are caring and you have a good nature and you're easy with people... most of the time. This is a new role and I think you are a perfect fit for it."

"What? You mean you want me to ... to." I was still lost for words, the only thing I could summon up was to start pointing in different directions in an effort to mime the locations I'd visited and the different Saints and Angels I'd met: "... to... to...".

"Yes, I want you to be a guide. Michael will be your superior, you both get on really well. He speaks highly of you, everyone you've met has. It is the job you were right for.

People always told you to become something where you helped others. You cared and entertained and put people at ease and could talk to someone, no matter their status in life or where they were born. I knew I had to choose someone who didn't just agree with me out of fear or what they could gain but because it was in their heart. At the end of the day it's what any parent wants from their children."

"I don't know what to say", I still struggled with the concept of what God wanted me to do but also how to thank him.

"I know you thought I was a mean old man, who just wanted you punished." He laughed.

Yet again I felt embarrassed.

"Well ... yes."

"Don't you think the God who invented laughter would have a sense of humour himself? Hmm. I just needed to make sure you got a whistle stop tour of the place and that you were as good as I thought you were."

"Really?"

"If some of the things you said with Lucifer were anything to go by you could maybe use a little more compassion in some areas. Remember you are not here to judge. You will learn in time. All it takes is time and the correct environment, that's all it takes anyone."

"Point taken, I'll bear that in mind. What I have come to realise since my time here is that love is the secret. You know if people cared for each other more we would solve most, if not all of the world's problems and how much of an amazing place would that be to live in."

"I know, I was impressed with the way you stuck up for the human race in the conversations you had with me and my son. I think it's time I gave you this."

He gave me the package from under his arm: "Go ahead open it." I looked at him with a blank expression then I carefully unwrapped the parcel, only to find a navy blue robe.

"Go on, put it on", He smiled at me like a proud father watching his son put a graduation gown on.

I dropped the robe over my head and it fell around my body fitting perfectly. Just then I started to feel a total calmness coming over me as if every worry, every fear, every heartache was draining from me. The sensation started from my head and travelled right through my body and out through my toes. The feeling was amazing. "Thank you."

"Please don't thank me, everyone wears them after their induction." God then took a deep breath and his face suddenly filled with sadness.

"And now to business unfortunately, Vincent. I have to give you your first job now. The first is always the hardest, especially in certain circumstances."

"I don't know if I'm ready though", I shook my head, I'd only just got the role, I was still finding my way.

"I have faith in you Vincent, just as you have always had faith in me."

"You think I've always had faith in you even when I was on Earth?" I asked, my own thoughts flashing back to when we first met when I told God that I didn't know if He existed and wondered if it was all just a dream.

"Of course. You might not have believed in me as a person or an entity but the kingdom of God is here within you. Blessed are those pure at heart for they should see God. You are pure of heart. Religion is really about that one thing. It doesn't matter what name you put on it or what religion you say you follow, it's the same for all religions. At the end of the day they are only words. It's only truly about caring for people and living honestly."

This statement really hit home to me. I had always tried to be kind and considerate and look after people and wanting justice where needed, I just didn't understand that it was all God expected from us.

His believing in me wasn't just about turning up at a church and saying that you believed in him, but was more loving yourself and the people around you regardless of who they were, what they looked like, their sexual orientation, the colour of their skin, whether they were weaker or stronger, smaller or taller, faster or slower physically, or mentally different. It was and always has been love, pure love.

"I don't know what to say", I started to feel different again as if I had just grown, as if some inner light was shining from my being, and it felt amazing.

"Please don't say a thing; your face says it all. Now here we are at the collection point." We had walked up to a single level building and in front of a pair of white double doors. "The job is yours now Vincent, but know that you are never alone. We are all here if you need us at any time. We are all on the same side and just like one big family."

"Thank you for the confirmation... Father." I opened one of the doors to walk through and for the first time in a very long time I felt as though I was somewhere I belong.

"Oh, and Vince", God said.

I stopped in my tracks and turned around, at the same time realising it was the first time He had called me by the shortened version of my name.

"It's good to have you here and please look after her." God smiled, winked at me then walked off.

The doors swung to a close behind me. I realised that I was near the same place I had first appeared. I turned around to see the entrance to the office where I had initially met Michael and Peter. Everything still felt as though it was buzzing around in my mind; everything that had happened since I'd been there, the people, the tests and especially the last conversation with God.

I sat down on one of the white plastic seats, and looking around I realised the place resembled an airport terminal. The white plastic seats with little tables around them, and even the top of the escalator that I first came up.

The escalator constantly moved around in motion and I watched it for what seemed like ages. After a while I suddenly got a feeling someone was coming up, my instinct was correctly predicted as a top of a head appeared upon the slow moving escalator. I stood up as the whole person came into view. The person, a woman, had her back facing towards me as she looked down the escalator towards the direction where she must have come from, trying to get her bearings.

I walked towards her; she suddenly turned around as the escalator placed her softly onto the floor once she had reached the top. We both stared at each other for a moment.

"Jennifer", I said softly.

"Vincent", she said astonished.

I smiled: "Yeah petal, it's me."

She rushed into my arms and we held each other.

"Oh Vince, there has been a terrible car crash."

"Yeah, I know."

"You know, how?" Her head craned back to look into my eyes.

I laughed slightly.

"Let's just say someone who cares just... this moment told me. Are you okay?"

"Yes... I... I'm fine, but how can you be here … you … you died on the day you proposed to me?"

"Yeah, I know, I did, I mean... I am. I'm sorry I left you by yourself and went away."

"But if you're here and I'm here then does that mean …" Jennifer fought with herself to say the words but she probably couldn't bring herself to even think it let alone say it.

"I'm afraid so", I held her tighter. "Please don't be scared. There's nothing to be scared of, honestly. I'm here to look after you. It's like paradise here. Come on."

I took Jennifer's hand tenderly and led her towards the entrance of the reception where Peter would be working.

"But where are we going?" she asked.

"I've got some pretty amazing things to show you. You'll love it", I beamed.

"Nice robes by the way Where did you get them from?"

"They're a present from a very dear friend of mine", I smiled.

"I've missed you so much Vince, I love you."

I opened the door for us both to step through.

"Hey do you still want to get married?"

"I'd love to Vince, but God knows who will marry us here."

"Well, He does owe me a favour."

ABOUT THE AUTHOR

Lee Brown was born in Newcastle upon Tyne but now lives in Northampton. He has held down several jobs, his first as a civil servant before becoming a computer programmer and worked for several large organisations such as The Times and St John Ambulance. He sometimes frequents the stand-up circuit in London and at the moment writing a television sitcom and a movie script.

Visit his website at www.averybritishafterlife.co.uk

Printed in Germany
by Amazon Distribution
GmbH, Leipzig